Finally, though, patience paid off for Travis Cobb. Chance Cooper's slim figure left the cover of the live oaks and approached the other shadowy figure.

"You see him, Morg?" Cooper asked. "I figured for certain he was behind me."

"Could've run," Delaney answered. "Or he could be watchin' the both o' us right now."

The two killers dove to cover the instant Travis fired. His bullet nicked Cooper's ankle, and the young gunman shouted a fair collection of curses in reply.

"You're a dead man now, Cobb," Cooper said. "We got you marked."

Delamer Westerns by G. Clifton Wisler
*Published by Fawcett Gold Medal Books:*

# SAM DELAMER

## G. Clifton Wisler

FAWCETT GOLD MEDAL • NEW YORK

*In loving memory of
C. S. Higgins,
teller of tales*

# CHAPTER 1

Texas, that late summer of 1868, seemed a sea of despair. Robert E. Lee had surrendered at Appomattox Courthouse more than three years before, but the peace the ragtag Confederates had hoped would follow proved elusive. Even now bluecoat garrisons occupied ports and cities, and local governments were superseded by federal judges appointed on the basis of adherence to Republican party dogma, not because they had a knowledge of the law or an interest in justice.

Those were bitter times. While garrison commanders, federal appointees, and the state government accrued personal fortunes, the people languished under the heavy yoke of stiff taxes. For many, like the former Confederate cavalryman Travis Cobb and his neighbor, ex-captain Sam Delamer, life was a daily struggle to keep alive the prewar hopes and promises while avoiding the ire of occupation and taxation.

"Worst part is payin' out these taxes to a bunch o' Yanks and watchin' our own people, who need our help so bad, go wantin' for bread and shelter," Travis often remarked to his brother Lester. "And we can't even cast a vote against it!"

"Ballots wouldn't mean much anyway," young Les argued. "Only thing gets listened to is gold and greenbacks. And bullets."

Travis frowned at such talk. It was hard to explain to Les, who hadn't shared the long starving months in the Richmond and Petersburg trenches or the haunted nights at Shiloh and in the Wilderness, listening to the cries of the wounded, that guns never settled a thing. When had the regiment ever lost a fight? And yet they'd stacked their arms with the rest at Appomattox and returned home defeated.

All save Willie. When the rest of the Texans tramped their way to the railroad junction to accept ole Grant's promise of free transport to New Orleans and hence to Galveston, Willie'd only laughed.

"We know the way home, don't we, boys?" he'd called. Even after four hard years fighting, Willie Delamer wasn't beaten. They'd set off on horses near starved to bones, with only side arms and a few Yank greenbacks to stave off starvation. In no time the horses had fattened themselves on good grass, and new rifles were come by courtesy of an unguarded federal depot. It had taken almost a year to reach the Brazos. Disease and renegades had whittled down the company some. Even so, Willie got them home.

"But to what?" Travis mumbled as he formed a knot in his string tie and glanced at the clean-shaven image in the looking glass. For once his dark hair was trimmed neatly, and his old boots sported a fresh coat of bootblack buffed to a sheen by little Davy, the seven-year-old brother too young to recall the high talk that had sent Travis off to battle. No, the younger Cobbs knew only the sour taste of defeat and occupation.

"Cheer up, son," old Arthur Cobb called from the doorway. "Anybody didn't know better'd say you were bound for a funeral and not a weddin'! Come have a glance at your sister. Never looked so pretty in all her life!"

Travis struggled to match his father's grin. It wasn't pos-

2

sible. For in a sense Ellen's wedding *was* a funeral. Even now, as she prepared to exchange vows with Dr. Jackson Trent of Decatur, there was a faraway look in her eyes. She, too, was perhaps remembering Willie Delamer. And when Travis stepped out and gripped her hand, she whispered, "I know. I wish he was here, too."

That was the whole trouble, Travis thought. Willie should have been there. He would have been the one to wed Ellen. They'd all known it as youngsters racing ponies along the river. Friends, neighbors, brothers really. That was what Travis Cobb always figured. But for Sam, it would have been. How does a man buy his own brother's death? That question broke Willie Delamer's soul, stole his resolve, buried his future.

"I think of him a lot, you know," Travis told his sister as he steadied her quivering hand.

"If only he hadn't died," she said, sighing. "Enough of that!" she then scolded herself. "Jack's a good man, and he'll be a better husband and father than a woman has a right to expect these days. I'm fortunate to have him."

Travis nodded his agreement. Yet Willie's ghost seemed at hand, spreading a pall over the scene. Travis dared not tell Ellen he might be alive even now. Willie'd made them promise, Trav and Les and the others, that they would attest to his death.

"I can never go back, don't you see?" Willie had told them somberly. "If I did, I'd wind up killing Sam. How can a man bring on death to his own blood?"

"That's a question Sam ought to answer," Travis had responded. "It should haunt him every waking moment!" Travis thought so even now.

Sam Delamer *was* a haunted man. And it *was* the face of his younger brother William that plagued him. Willie's easy grin, his natural feel for the land, his way with horses, his gift for rallying men to his side; they were all envied. In the

3

end, it was that boyish idealism of Willie's that had undone him. Major Willie Delamer, Confederate hero, who never met a horse or a man he couldn't win over! Fool brother never understood the Trident Ranch was a battlefield, too, and that only one Delamer could rule the place. As for the other . . .

"Dear, I thought you paid to have this road improved," Sam's wife Helen complained as she ducked under a live-oak branch that threatened to block the path.

"Oh, we pay that Yank judge for lots of things," Sam grumbled. "Few of them ever get done. I'll send someone out to clear that limb. Can't have the Cobbs' path to town obstructed, can we?"

In truth, Sam had blocked that road a half-dozen times. Then Willie had come riding in like a phantom to guarantee the Cobbs free passage to market. Willie, who would have settled for living in that old dog-run cabin down on the river! Now the Cobbs had a signed agreement, and they remained, like a thorn in Sam's side, surrounded by Trident acreage that otherwise would have choked them into surrender.

"It's a fine man Ellen's found herself for a husband," Helen declared. "A doctor! In truth, I thought she would surely pine away her best years in sorrow over your brother William."

"Made herself ill," Sam explained. "Was near dying as I heard it. This Dr. Trent turned her fever, and she took him to heart. As for Willie, that was all girlish nonsense."

"I suppose," Helen said, sighing. "Still, people speak of it differently."

"What people? Bunch of back-pew gossips. She hardly knew Willie once he was grown. War turned him vicious, you know. You remember how he shot that cavalry major out by the barn his first night back. Lucky the Yanks didn't hang him for it. It's best he headed into the wilds. No place here for a killer."

"Yes, dear," Helen said, resting her head on Sam's bulky shoulder.

They arrived at the gate of the Cobb ranch a few moments later. The younger boys, fifteen-year-old Jesse and thirteen-year-old Bobby, greeted them with cold glares. Strange how different the youngsters looked, all scrubbed and dandied, with their hair trimmed and the scraggly whiskers razored off their chins. But beneath it all, the familiar hostility lingered.

"Well, look here, Pa!" young Edna Cobb called. The eleven-year-old gazed at Sam with wonderment. The girl was the image of Ellen, bright-eyed and lithe, and she was entirely frozen by the sparkling pearl necklace Helen Delamer wore around her neck.

"Let me give you a hand there, Miz Delamer," Art Cobb offered. "Surprised to see you, ma'am, what with the birthing only a week ago and all."

"It's her first time off the ranch since little Stephen came into the world," Sam explained. "I argued against it, but you all know Helen. There's not a wedding or a christening she knows about that we're not there."

"Beginnings, you know," Helen said as she took old Art's hand and descended from the carriage. "My mother always thought it a duty, even where the colored folk were concerned. Many's the time I watched a pair of darkies jump the broom."

Her amusement was not matched by the Cobbs, and Sam drew her aside.

"Fine thing," rancher Ted Slocum muttered. "Comparin' Ellie's weddin' to a matin' o' slaves!"

"More or less the same where a Delamer's concerned," Les Cobb answered loudly. "Just no-accounts to be moved about, bought and sold."

Travis led his brother away, and Sam breathed a sigh of relief.

"It wasn't what Helen meant at all," Sam told Art. "We would never bring offense to such old friends."

"It's forgotten," Art said, his eyes betraying the sting. "Hard on a new mother to leave a child so soon. There's the nursin' and all to bear in mind."

"Oh, we have help for such things," Helen explained. "It's best children are left to those who have the patience."

"Sure," Art said coldly.

They continued on inside the Cobbs' house. As was typical along the frontier, the building had evolved over time from a single-room cabin to a dog-run—two twinned rooms separated by a covered porch, thence to a two-story farmhouse, with extra rooms added as time passed and the family increased. The center of the house now formed a family quarters, and it was there that Ellen Cobb waited for the Methodist circuit minister to begin the ceremony.

Across the room stood Dr. Jackson Trent, the bridegroom. Sam Delamer eyed the doctor with amusement. Trent wasn't a thing like Willie. Taller and stiff-backed, the doc spoke with a formal flavor, and he seemed at ease in the crowded room.

"Dr. Trent, my name's Sam Delamer," Sam introduced himself. "This paragon of beauty on my arm is my wife Helen. We wish you every good fortune."

"Thank you," the doctor responded, bowing to Helen as he gripped Sam's hand politely. "I've heard a great deal about your family. In particular about your late lamented brother Will."

"Yes," Sam muttered. "He was a man to attract attention."

The doctor seemed anxious to talk more, but at that moment Sam noticed a pair of new arrivals. One was a young government clerk, Pat Tyler, whose family had suffered for its Union sympathies during the war. Now the Tylers were reaping the benefits of those sympathies.

Accompanying the clerk was a round-faced Ohioan, former congressman and state senator DeWitt Fulton. Fulton ruled a fifth of Texas from his courtroom in Jacksboro. As federal judge, he was virtual ruler over a hundred miles in any direction.

"Hello, Sam," Fulton called. "It's been a while since we've seen you."

"Been busy," Sam answered the grinning judge. "You know my wife Helen."

"I understand congratulations are in order," Fulton said, kissing Helen's limp hand. "Another boy, was it?"

"We named him Stephen," Helen answered. "After Sam's brother killed by the Indians years ago."

"You lost one of your own that way, too, didn't you?" the judge noted. "It's said a hundred Comanches paid for that boy with their hides."

"Would have been a hundred more if we'd caught them," Sam said bitterly. "It's what happens to those who tangle with me."

"Ah, some would take that for a warning, Sam," Fulton said, smiling as he glanced around at the various Cobbs.

"Some might," Sam said, resting his eyes on the judge.

"Sam, dear, it appears they're ready to begin," Helen observed, pointing to where old Art was positioning the minister. "Let's find a good spot. You know how I love to see it all."

"Excuse us," Sam said, making way for his wife as he cut through the crowd.

"We'll be talking more soon," Judge Fulton promised.

Sam could only guess at the Ohioan's meaning. Even so, the words held an ominous tone.

The wedding was brief but rather stylish for such doings on the frontier. Helen remarked at the lace attached to Ellen's hems and cuffs, and the Cobbs had barbecued a steer, a prize hog, and several chickens. Platters of fruits and vegetables were brought outside and placed on long tables. Young Bobby strummed a guitar, and Art did a fair job with his fiddle. In

7

no time lively music set the company to dancing, those who weren't too busy eating, that is. And while the happy couple received their guests' best wishes, the younger Cobb boys engaged in a bit of mischief, setting off firecrackers and peppering their elders with rice or popcorn.

Jack Trent eventually led his bride to a table, and the newlyweds enjoyed their first meal as man and wife. Les and Travis saw their needs were met. Then Inez Flores, who cooked for the Slocum ranch down on the Clear Fork of the Brazos, brought forth a wondrous three-tiered cake, and the company applauded.

"It's best Jack do the cutting," Ellen announced. "He's the surgeon, after all."

"Sure, dear, but I never cut on anything that doesn't get sewed up afterward."

"Doesn't get a bill to pay, you mean," Art said, and the crowd laughed. In the end, Ellen and her new husband cut the cake together.

"Wherever did they come by enough sugar to bake such a cake!" Helen remarked as she swallowed her first bite. "This doctor must have money."

"More likely was Slocum," Sam decided. "He and Travis served together in the war."

"With your brother, too? Why is it none of your wartime companions happen along with such generosity, Sam?"

"Not too many made it back," Sam explained. "And after all, I was an officer. The man who issues commands isn't as apt to make friends of his men."

"Wasn't William . . ."

"I answered you, Helen!" Sam barked. "You've always had all the sugar and everything else, for that matter, that you needed or wanted. I never asked my friends for help. Delamers never need it."

"Yes, Sam," she said, turning to seek the minister's ear. Sam, meanwhile, was taken off to the opposite side by DeWitt Fulton.

"I'm rather surprised you haven't come into town for a visit of late," Fulton said.

"I told you I've been occupied," Sam retorted.

"Well, of course, but the child didn't keep you from this wedding. I never knew you to be on good terms with the Cobb family. As I recall . . ."

"They're neighbors," Sam said, fighting to hold back the anger at being pressed by the two-bit politician. "I planned to come into Jacksboro before September, though."

"It might be that would be too late. I've made some plans, Sam. Big ones. A man like you, one with men on his payroll and high plans of his own, might prove of assistance."

"Go on, Judge."

"The occupation, after all, won't last forever. I don't doubt that as soon as the president is satisfied Texas has set aside her rebelious sympathies, he will remove all but the frontier troops. And, after all, what use is the cavalry for enforcing order? They can't even put an end to these raiding Comanches! Jack County alone has lost a fortune in stolen beeves and horses. I myself barely escaped with my hair a month ago when the brazen heathens attacked my surveying crew."

"Building more roads?" Sam asked, chuckling to himself.

"That's progress, isn't it?" the judge said slyly. "It's why we need more tax revenues."

"Is it?" Jackson Trent asked, joining the discussion. "I'd think the roads could wait a bit, Judge Fulton. I see so much suffering, like at Fleatown, as we call the camps outside Decatur inhabited by war widows and orphans, not to mention freedmen unable to find work. I wish you'd use a little of those generous taxes for medicine to treat the unfortunates. Or for food to feed the orphans."

"I must tell you, doctor, there's little sympathy for the spawn of Rebels in Washington, or in Austin, either, for that matter. You Southerners speak of granting pensions to men who fought to bring down the Union! Aren't the soldiers

9

garrisoned in your towns enough of a reminder that your cause is lost?''

''Are the people to be lost as well?'' Trent asked. ''It would seem a starving child has little use for politics. A bit of cornmeal and some bacon might keep him alive, though. Your own soldiers bring us stray beeves sometimes, or shoot a few buffalo. Why is it those charged with the responsibility can't do more?''

''What soldiers have done this?'' the judge asked. ''All captured cattle are to be brought under the authority of my court.''

''Then I guess we know what'll become of 'em, don't we?'' Travis asked, laughing. ''Don't waste your breath, Jack. These carpetbaggers have deep pockets. They only hear the likes o' Sam Delamer.''

''That's enough!'' Pat Tyler shouted. ''You've brought this plague down on Texas. Those of you who flocked to Rebel colors and turned your back on Sam Houston back in sixty-one. How many of you have empty rooms and full corncribs? You take in the widows and orphans.''

Silence settled over the crowd for a moment. Then Art Cobb took up his fiddle, and the anger passed away. The dancing resumed, and Judge Fulton sadly shook his head.

''They'll never understand what's best for them, will they, Sam?'' Fulton asked.

''Never will,'' Sam echoed, biting his lip. ''As for now, I'd best collect Helen and get her along home. She's not yet strong, you understand.''

''Oh, I understand, Sam. More than you perhaps do. Come see me soon, won't you? I've a notion we can come to terms that will be equally rewarding.''

''I'm sure. Soon,'' Sam promised.

The judge chuckled to himself as Sam left.

''Worst kind of parasite,'' Sam mumbled as he hurried toward Helen. And there wasn't a thing that could be done. Well, not that didn't incur high risks anyway.

He paused long enough to unfold a pair of telegrams he'd received only that morning. The first was from a Pinkerton agent in the Dakotas.

"EX-REBEL AS YOU DESCRIBED FOUND DEAD BIG HORNS. KILLED BY SIOUX. REMAINS SCALPED. POSITIVE IDENTITY IMPOSSIBLE."

"Impossible!" Sam said, grinding his teeth as he stuffed the telegram into his coat pocket. How many former Confederate cavalrymen could there be in the Big Horn country? The second message was more to Sam's liking.

"EN ROUTE. ARRIVE SOON. DELANEY."

So, Morgan Delaney would soon be at the Trident Ranch. Morg had experience bringing difficult folks to heel. Midnight Morgan, they called him on the Colorado. Maybe Delaney would drop in on the judge, too.

"Helen, it's time we started back," Sam declared as he greeted his wife.

"It's been delightful seeing you all again," Helen said, making her exit. "You must come out and visit the baby. Soon."

"Yes, soon," Judge Fulton said, nodding to Sam. "Very soon."

# CHAPTER 2

Ψ

Sam Delamer drove the carriage slowly homeward. Even so, the wheels didn't avoid every rock or rut, and Helen occasionally cried out as she was jarred about.

"You should have stayed at the house," Sam told her. "It was too soon."

"It would have been months before I had such a chance at company," Helen argued.

"Company?" he asked. "Bunch of dirt scratchers and cow chasers. They're not fit company for you or me, either."

"Then why did you go yourself?"

"It was expected, I suppose."

"I'd judge it was quite unexpected, dear. I thought for a moment Travis Cobb would faint dead away. We've had finer welcomes."

"Suppose we have," he said, laughing. "And we will have again."

"Oh?"

"This occupation nonsense won't last forever, Helen. Up ahead is a future as bright as any you knew in the old days back in New Orleans."

"You think so even now, with the world turned upside down?"

"Upside down? No, it just seems like that from where you look. Things have been moved around a little, but that's just because my father miscalculated some. It's excusable. The whole of the South did the same fool thing."

The last two miles of the journey Sam shifted the subject to the landscape, to the relentless churning of the river and the meandering streams that seemed to vanish each summer. It was growing hot, and even the canvas canopy overhead did little to deflect the furious rays of the Texas sun.

"Not far now, Helen," Sam seemed to remark every hundred yards. "Worst part of Texas, this heat. But it means mild winters."

"Since when?" she complained. "We had a foot and a half of snow last January, and the well froze in March. March! I sometimes wish you weren't so set on building this ranch, Sam. The climate in New Orleans is so much more pleasant, and Brother writes that the shipping business is better than ever."

**That why he scribbles me a new plea for a loan every week?** Sam wondered. He knew, however, Helen was sensitive about the matter, and he didn't speak his feelings.

Once they arrived at the house, Sam turned Helen over to her maid and ordered a bath made ready.

"That will cool you off, dear," he assured her. As for himself, he had Matthew, the house steward, prepare a brandy. Sipping it slowly, Sam ventured into the ranch office and gazed at the big map affixed to the wall. In its center the Brazos River wound its way through seven Texas counties. Northeast there stood Jacksboro and the federal post at Fort Richardson. West lay the next cavalry post, Fort Griffin, and the buffalo hunters' hovel known variously as The Flat or Fort Griffin Town. It might have been deemed both an embarrassment and a hazard to a big rancher. Sam found it a convenient source of cheap labor—especially the young, des-

13

perate sort who didn't ask many questions or have a lot of scruples.

It was at The Flat Sam first met Chance Cooper. Young Chance had been a rare find—quick-witted and completely fearless, with an instinct for survival. More than once the twenty-year-old had attended to some errand or other on a moonless night.

"You be needing anything else, Mr. Sam?" Matthew called from the doorway.

Sam turned and gazed a moment at the map. Then he stepped to the door and handed the servant his empty brandy snifter.

"Tell one of the boys to fetch Chance Cooper," Sam said somberly.

"Might be he gone to town," Matthew said, lowering his gaze when Sam turned his attention that way.

"Then have somebody ride to town and tell him," Sam added. "I don't care if he went to Austin. Have him fetched."

"Yes, sir, Mr. Sam," Matthew agreed as he hastily departed.

"Worst thing about these freedmen," Sam mumbled to himself as he returned to the office. "Too long being slaves left them witless. Won't make a move without me spelling it out."

But having Negro servants reminded Helen of her childhood along the Mississippi Delta, and the nurse who was looking after Stephen, Essie Sharp, was a wonder. Essie could hold that baby every waking moment and never tire of its soiled linen or squawling. In point of fact, there wasn't much crying, for Essie had her magic to cure each fit of temper.

Sam's digression was ended by a knock on the open door.

"You sent for me, Colonel?" Chance Cooper asked. Sam nodded, and the young man stepped inside the office. His denim trousers were caked with dried mud and dust, and his face was lined with sweat streaks.

14

"Close the door, Chance," Sam instructed.

"Came right away," Chance said as he secured the door. "Sorry to be such a state. Me and some o' the boys were out workin' horses. Awful hot out there."

"I don't pay you to wash," Sam declared. "Hot, you say. Hot enough for a fire?"

"Oh, we've been battlin' grass fires a week now, Colonel. Lost the west line shack in the last one."

"Fire, huh?" Sam said, drawing a line with his index finger along the fenced Trident acreage. Near the center was a box, an unsightly blemish on the expanding ranch.

"That's the Cobb place, ain't it?" Chance said, grinning. "We had our share o' run-ins with them folks. Even the little ones get sassy when they see that Trident brand on our horses. Be a pleasure to bring 'em down a notch or two, Colonel."

"Ever hear why we let them stay, Chance?" Sam asked. "Why we don't strangle them proper by damming the creeks and cutting the market road?"

"There's talk ole man Cobb's got himself a paper you signed," Chance said quietly. "Signed at gunpoint, some say. Was your pa's notion maybe."

"My brother's," Sam grumbled.

"Little Jamie? Can't see him botherin' you much."

"I had another brother, Chance."

"Oh, I heard o' him. Folks say he was taken with the Cobb girl what got herself married today. He's dead, ain't he?"

"Wasn't then. I needed him, and the Cobbs, too. It wasn't a gun held to my head, Chance. It was need got my name scrawled on that blamed paper."

"But you wouldn't mind it much if somethin' happened to that paper, eh?"

"If something did, we could cut off those Cobbs from town and water. With this heat we've got, it wouldn't take long to force their hand."

"Man who got rid o' that paper might make himself some money, wouldn't you say, Colonel?"

"Two hundred dollars for the fire. Another two hundred when they sell out."

"Four hundred's such a, well, untidy number. Wouldn't five round things off better."

"Five if it's done tonight," Sam agreed. "I'm in a mood to rid myself of some pests."

"Yes, sir," Chance said, grinning. "Don't you worry, either. I'll use dry brush so there's no coal-oil smell to warn 'em, and I'll do the whole thing personal."

"See Cobb doesn't save that paper," Sam insisted.

"Oh, I'll burn it first, Colonel."

"It's inside the house, in the top drawer of a rolltop desk."

"You know a lot o' things, don't you, Colonel? Makes a man prideful to know he's in such high company. I'll tend to it for you."

"They've got dogs," Sam warned.

"I got somethin' for 'em. Mix it with some beef, and them dogs won't trouble nobody."

"Do it up proper, Chance."

"Yes, sir, Colonel Delamer. I know my business. You rest easy. Tomorrow mornin' be some sad news comin' from the neighbors."

"Just make sure it's sad news for them."

"I aim to," Chance said, narrowing his eyes. "One thing you always know dealin' with me, Colonel. I be dead 'fore I'd give a boss cause to regret signin' me on. I owe you, sir. You fished me out o' that trouble over to The Flat. Like as not they'd stretched my neck, and for nothin' save protectin' my interests in a crooked card game!"

"Do it careful, and we'll have no need to save you a second time."

"I learn from my mistakes, you know. No sense to shootin' a man in a crowded place with plenty o' folks to swear it was a murder. Nobody asks questions on the back roads once the sun goes down."

"Makes life worth living, doesn't it, Chance?"

"Yes, sir," the young man said, grinning.

Sam drew out four crisp Yankee fifty-dollar notes and passed them to Cooper. The hireling then left the office, humming an old ditty and appearing in rare good humor.

Alone in the office, Sam gazed at the big fireplace. Above it, securely bolted, hung the ancient sword his grandfather had brought to Texas. It had belonged to *his* grandfather, a French nobleman, the Chevalier de Lyon. No one knew what surname he'd carried when he happened to save the life of young King Louis XV. The date and event were etched in the long, gleaming blade. Sam's great-grandfather, rather than discard that fool sword, had fled the revolution aboard ship, carrying along a young son who was to become Will Delamer. *De la mer.* Of the sea, those refugees had called themselves, for noble heads were falling right and left in Paris, and Louisiana provided refuge.

There was another sword up there, too, the fine-tempered blade given by the New Orleans Grays to the Texas captain that accompanied them to death and glory at Goliad. Big Bill Delamer had retrieved that sword from a Mexican colonel at San Jacinto.

For the longest time, back at the small cabin down on the Brazos, a third sword had hung over the fireplace. It was the blade given Big Bill by the Republic of Texas and later carried by him in the Mexican War. Willie had taken possession of that sword when their father fell at Shiloh back in '62. Like as not, it now decorated some Sioux lodge!

It didn't matter. There was too much of Big Bill in that house already. He'd scratched a home out of the wilderness, true enough, and he'd been a celebrated leader of men. But he never accumulated a fourth of the acreage Sam had added. He'd been soft with the Indians, too!

Colonel Bill Delamer! Colonel! People now called Sam by that title, in spite of the fact that he'd never held commission as more than a captain of cavalry, and that had been short-lived. The title was inherited, just like the ranch. No, that had been taken, earned by toil and blood, pried from brother Willie's fingers through cunning and resolve.

"Sure, you'd have another sword or two up there, wouldn't you, Brother? A cavalry saber. Or maybe a tomahawk."

That was Willie. Run off to live with the Comanches. Run off and play soldier while Sam fought to keep the ranch from dying of neglect. For so long Sam had envied Willie the good looks, the grace on horseback, the courage that sent him in and out of battles while Sam had fled the single instance he witnessed combat.

"Why stay and die?" he'd asked himself a thousand times. "What use is glory to a corpse?"

The war had buried a million idealists. Now was the time for other men, those like Sam Delamer, men willing to do what was required to survive.

"I spend a lot of time wondering what manner of snake hires his own brother's killin'," Travis Cobb once told Sam.

"Willie got in my way," Sam had answered. "Don't you go and make the same mistake, Cobb!"

It was a ruthless game, this scramble for power. One day that map would all be Delamer land, every acre of it. Oh, it might take a few fires and a few bullets, but it would come to pass. And Sam Delamer would be there to make sure.

Sam glanced over the ranch accounts, taking care to delete the two hundred dollars paid Chance Cooper. "Title transfer expenses," he described it. Then, content there was nothing more to attend to, Sam left the office and set off to have a look after the children.

They were his delight and joy, those little ones. One might perhaps grow strong enough to be a governor or senator. The Trident would wield that kind of power in a few more years.

"Papa," three-year-old Catherine called, hurrying into her father's arms. Sam doted on the girl, and he lifted her onto one shoulder and continued on into the small courtyard which was given over to the youngsters most afternoons. Tall oaks offered some shade, but the sun had turned the boys, Robert and Sam, Jr., into a pair of sandy-haired mops.

"Papa, will you take us down to the river for a swim?" Robert asked. At eight, his hair was darkening, but he still appeared too frail and fragile for the hard life ahead. Sam, only five, promised to be stouter, like his father. Sam Delamer stood six feet tall and spread a taut two hundred pounds on a solid frame.

"They swim naked in the river," Catherine whispered.

"Better to soak yourselves in a tub," Sam announced. "Been too many strangers riding by of late for you to habit the river. Maybe later we'll share a game of checkers."

"Or chess?" Robert asked eagerly. "I beat Matthew regularly now, Papa."

"Better give yourself a few years before taking on the master," Sam advised.

"You could show me some moves, like Uncle Jamie does. Even let me win."

"It's a bad lesson you'd learn from that, Robert," Sam argued. "Outside, in the world beyond the Trident, nobody will let you win. Learn your own moves. Develop your own strategy. And never give your own away. Feint and deception. Those are the keys."

"Yes, sir," Robert said, dropping his chin onto his chest. "I just thought since you love to play so much . . ."

"Practice. Maybe soon we'll have a match."

Robert nodded, then set off toward the door. Little Sam followed, pausing every few steps to tie a shoe or examine a pebble.

"Papa, can we go and see the baby now?" Catherine asked.

"Just for a bit," he said, allowing Catherine to climb down and lead the way toward the nursery. Stephen rested in Essie's big hands as she swayed back and forth in an old oak rocker. Catherine walked over quietly and peeked at her little brother. The baby was asleep, and Sam led her back to the courtyard.

"Play awhile, then get along and have a bath yourself," Sam told her. "Tell one of the maids when you're ready, but do it before supper."

Catherine nodded, though Sam knew the girl had no sense of time and place. Matthew had pointed out once that few three-year-olds did, but Charlie had known. Moreover, Sam had shown his considerable resentment at the black man's presumption.

Charlie! Sam could never gaze at the children without remembering the cherub-faced child the Comanches had slain. The arrow might have taken Robert instead, or even baby Sam. But instead it sought out Charlie, the spry three-year-old who was forever exploring and venturing and daring. While Robert huddled with the baby behind the oak table, Charlie had been handing powder cartridges to Jamie. Then the arrow flew through the narrow slot in the heavy shutter used for firing at the raiders.

"Papa?" the astonished boy had called. Then, as blood poured from his chest, Charlie fell to the floor and died in a shudder of bewildered agony. And Sam? He'd been elsewhere.

"Sam?" Helen called as she approached down the narrow hall. "Sam, are you all right?"

"Yes," he said, swallowing his pain. "Just remembering."

"Not Charlie again," she said, sadly shaking her head. "I thought the baby might salve that memory."

"Nothing ever will," he argued. "He's here every minute."

"Well, perhaps this would be a good time to go east. We could visit my family and show the little ones a taste of civilization. Don't say no."

"My dear, when did I ever deny you the opportunity to travel. Take the children along if you choose."

"And you?"

"I've got business to attend to," he told her.

"The Cobbs?"

He nodded, and she scowled.

"I thought after going to the wedding and all, you might have set that thought aside," Helen told him.

"I never in my life left anything important untended, Helen. You know me well enough to have observed that."

"People change sometimes, Sam."

"Some do. They lack the will to stand by a thing."

"And you?"

"I set my course and stick to it."

# CHAPTER 3

Travis Cobb nervously paced back and forth along the porch of the house. In the distance the dust raised from Jack Trent's carriage rose in a single plume, marking Ellen's departure to her future home in Decatur. Travis would miss her. She'd always been his sounding board, his second soul. Ellie had shared those better days of childhood, swimming and fishing the river, racing ponies with Willie, growing taller and wiser as they discovered the mysteries of life.

"Lord, Willie, where've you gotten to?" Travis whispered to the wind. Once there would have been an answer, even if it was a stirring of the breeze or a sensation. Now there was nothing. "Guess maybe you really are dead," Travis said, feeling the chill that accompanied the thought. If still alive, Willie would have returned. Nothing, not all the Yank brigades and cannonballs in Virginia, kept him from coming back from the war. His heart was in that place, and his soul would never belong far from the river.

That's how it is with me, too, Travis thought. But it was a bitter hard day that found Travis Cobb in that place alone, without the two people who had shared his dreams all those years ago. Loneliness haunted a man, even one with brothers and a father to share the struggles of life.

"The other boys took off to have 'emselves a swim in the creek," Arthur Cobb told his oldest son upon stepping out onto the porch. "Grown too old for such foolishness?"

"No, Pa," Travis said, managing a trace of a smile. "Just now, though, I don't seem to have the heart for it."

"Missin' her already, huh? Well, I felt the same for your ma. Be an empty place with her and Ellie both gone now."

"Yes, sir."

"Had another offer on the farm, you know."

"From Sam Delamer?" Travis asked, tensing.

"No, from that Tyler pup. Said he's actin' for a private interest, but . . ."

"He clerks for Judge Fulton," Travis grumbled. "We know who's tight with that crook, don't we? Good thing we did well with the trail herd this year. We'll be able to pay whatever new tax he comes upon."

"You know I gave Ellie five hundred dollars to get herself settled into a house."

"Yes, sir," Travis said, grinning. Hadn't he drawn the bank draft himself?

"I got some put away for the boys, enough to see 'em started out right."

"Pa, I think you just lost me."

"Trav, I'm an old man, mostly worn down to a stub from fightin' Indians and Texas summers and Sam Delamer. The drive brought us enough cash to start that string of horses you and young Willie always thought to build."

"Willie's gone now, Pa."

"Still a need for horses, and plenty o' cheap land to the west. Ted Slocum and I had a talk 'bout it. Two thousand dollars would buy up that fine acreage just south o' him on the Clear Fork o' the Brazos. Good grazin' for longhorns, and any mustanger worth his feed could grab up a hundred

23

head in a year. As I said, always a need for horses hereabouts.''

''What're you sayin'? Sell this place?''

''Son, I had your ma buried in Palo Pinto, at the town plot. Know why?''

''No, sir,'' Travis said, shaking his head.

'' 'Cause I figured sooner or later Sam Delamer'd have this place. Couldn't stand the thought o' her restin' on his pasture. Maybe it's time you took Les and headed west, built a home for yourself. One without shadows lurkin' 'round to trouble you.''

''This is my home, Pa. I've bled for this land.''

''No, son. This is *my* home. When I'm dust-blowin' in a September norther, you'll still have years and years to ride this earth. Holdin' on means another fight, and I'm tired o' battlin' a man that never wearies.''

''Let Sam Delamer have the ranch?'' Travis cried. ''They'll bury me here first.''

''And Les? Jesse, Bobby, even little Edna and Davy. You saw Sam tonight, come to bless Ellen's weddin'. The feudin's done for a time. Maybe we should make sure it's done forever.''

''Not for long, Pa,'' Travis argued. ''I know Sam. You start worryin' when he goes to smilin' at you. This is a man paid to have his own brother shot. More'n likely had Willie killed. Rattlers give warnin', Pa. Snake to fear's the one grins at you while he sharpens his fangs.''

''What can he do, Trav? I got his signature on that paper in my desk. Long as we got it, he can't close the road or block our water. He's got to live with us. Unless we do the smart thing and clear out.''

''I can't believe you're sayin' this! Pa, you love this place more'n I do.''

''And I love my family even more,'' Art said, resting a wrinkled hand on Travis's shoulder. ''You learned about

24

fightin' battles you couldn't win in Virginia. Can't you see this here's one?''

"We won more'n we lost even then," Travis objected. "We'll win this one, too."

"Wish I was half as sure," Art said, frowning. "Now, what say we tackle that creek 'fore the boys have swum it empty."

"Go ahead, Pa. I'll look in on Edna."

"That girl's too busy dreamin' o' her own weddin' to give her fool family a thought. Come along, Trav. You need a wash."

"I do?" Travis asked, pulling the loose ends of his tie so that the bow vanished.

"Sure to cool you off," Art argued.

"Then let me kick off my boots and get into a pair o' overalls. I'll be along soon enough."

"Best not tarry. We'll have the creek emptied."

"Yes, sir," Travis said, turning toward the door and hurrying along to the room he shared with Les and Jesse.

It didn't take long to step out of his Sunday clothes and scramble into a pair of well-worn denim overalls. The outfit was a good deal more suitable to the fierce summer weather, and it wouldn't take a second to shed it and step into the cooling waters of the creek.

"You goin' down to the creek, too?" Edna asked as Travis headed for the door.

"Thought to," he answered. "Got chores for me, do you, Sis?"

"Somebody's got to clean up all the leavin's," she complained. "Not everybody can go splashin' 'round in the creek."

"Bet Sue Huntley'll be along tomorrow and chase you down there," Travis said, grinning as he wrapped an arm around the eleven-year-old. "Be hard bein' the only girl 'round this batch o' renegades. Maybe once Ellie gets settled some, you can head to Decatur for a visit."

"Think so?"

"Know it. She'll be hungry for the company, too, don't you figure? Sure won't want Bobby and Davy up there to keep out o' trouble."

"You won't need me to churn the butter or help with harvest?"

"We will be short some, but I guess you'll've earned a furlough from this outfit."

"You'll talk to Pa 'bout it?"

"Won't take a lot o' talkin', I'm thinkin'. We won't be too long, either, Edna," Travis promised. "Most likely you'll be glad the boys won't smell like the hogs' pen for a change."

"That's a thought," she said, matching his smile.

Travis hurried along to the creek then. His father was sitting on a stump watching Lester fend off an attack from the younger boys, and Travis gave the old man a nod before peeling off his overalls and splashing into the shallow stream. Instantly Jesse hurried over and began a splash fight, and the others quickly joined in. Travis tolerated the attention for a time, then reached out and snatched a brother in each arm and dragged them out into the deepest part of the channel.

"Time for a truce?" he asked, dunking Jesse under as he turned to little Bobby.

"Surrender'd be more like it!" Bobby exclaimed.

Jesse, half-drowned and coughing water from his lungs, wasn't in any position to argue. As for Les and Davy, they busied themselves elsewhere.

Later the brothers scrambled about a bit more, with Travis and Les racing Jesse a hundred yards from their father's toes to an overhanging willow tree. The younger ones had their own race, but neither swam well enough yet to trounce the other the way Les took Travis and Jesse.

"Good time to be alive, this," Art declared when Travis led the way out of the creek and onto the grassy knoll beyond. "Fine night this'll be. Sweet smell to the air."

"Honeysuckle," Les observed as he sniffed the air.

"Somethin' else, too," Jesse said, frowning. Travis followed the younger Cobb's eyes from the creek back toward the house. A narrow whiff of smoke seemed to thread its way skyward.

"Edna wouldn't have dinner cookin'," Art said, rising slowly. "Not with half a ham not eaten by the weddin' guests."

"She'd know better'n to burn green wood, too," Les added. "Smoke's growin' black. And the smell's . . ."

"Paint," Travis said, racing to his overalls and plunging his legs into them. "Hurry and get your trousers on, little brothers. We got a fire to fight!"

There was nothing so feared as a fire in late summer. Brush and trees were dry enough to flare up like winter tinder, and a wisp of wind could send a prairie blaze racing across half the county. The Cobbs rushed toward their house in near panic. Travis arrived first, screaming Edna's name and taking in the scene simultaneously.

"Here," the girl shouted, waving from the pump. Her thin arms worked frantically to fill a water bucket. Meanwhile Art raced on into the house itself. Jesse grabbed a spade and began beating at the flames spreading from the back of the house toward the barn.

"Pa!" Travis called, taking the half-full bucket from Edna and rushing into the house. Already the rooms were choked with smoke, and bright yellow flames devoured the kitchen.

"Lord, help us!" Les shouted as he formed his brothers into a bucket brigade and hurried a fresh pail of water toward Travis.

"Can't save the house, Pa!" Travis shouted as he threw water on the nearest wall. "Roof's already caught."

"Get the chests out of the front rooms then," Art instructed. "Knock out the windows and throw what you can outside. Shoes, beddin', linens, what's hard to come by."

"I'll do it," Travis promised. "Pa, you get yourself outside. You got no business eatin' all this smoke."

27

"Got to get the cash box," Art explained. "Now get along with you!"

It was a frantic race to see whether Travis could empty the rooms before the roof fell in and flames swallowed the Cobbs' scant possessions. Outside, Les and Jesse fought to clear the adjacent ground and stop the fire's spread. Even little Davy beat at flaming grass with a blanket, coughing as smoke blackened his face and ate at his lungs.

Travis, meanwhile, knocked out the bedroom windows and threw chests of clothes and linens outside. His father and Bobby dragged the rescued belongings to safety. There was no saving beds or the heavy oak table and chairs. The fire spread too quickly. Finally, as glass swelled and exploded, Travis leaped out the back room's solitary window and joined his distraught family.

"There goes a year and a half's labor," Les said, frowning as the center of the house imploded.

"What's been built can be put up again," Art argued. "Been burned out twice by Comanches, you know."

"Puttin' up a dog-run's one thing," Travis said, dropping to his knees and coughing smoke from his lungs. "Rebuildin' this place, well, be a long time gettin' it done."

"Least we saved the barn," Jesse said, mustering a smile. "And with the heat, it won't be so bad sleepin' outside."

"Freeze your tailbone come winter," Bobby said, laughing. "Sure was some good lemonade burned up, though."

"And the ham," Jesse complained. "I was sure hungry for it, too."

"It's still there," Les declared. "Might be a bit overcooked now, but you like it that way, don't you, Jess?"

"Not charcoal," Jesse muttered.

"I got to the desk," Art announced, holding up a small tin box. "Saved the cash."

"Never mind the cash," Travis said, shuddering as a cold sensation flooded his insides. "What about the paper."

"Should be here, too," Art said, opening the box. "It's

gone! Can't be! I put it right here on top of the corn contract. I couldn't've dropped it!"

"Must have, Pa," Les said, rushing toward the house. "Look 'round, boys! It must've fell out."

"No, it didn't," Travis said, biting his lip to hold in the anger swelling up inside him. "Edna, where'd the fire start?"

"In the floor," she said.

"In the floor?" Les asked. "Not by the stove or over by the chimney?"

"The stove was colder'n winter night," she insisted. "Nobody's had a fire in the fireplace since what, April? No, the first thing I saw was flames blazin' up from the floor. It was like the old devil himself come up from—"

"We get the notion, girl," Art interrupted. "Don't need to go blasphemin' now, do you?"

"No, sir."

"This fire was set," Travis declared, kicking a rock into the sea of burning embers that had shortly before been a home.

"Where's ole Buck?" Les asked. "How'd anybody get past that dog?"

"Easy," Bobby said, staring at several lumps near the barn. "All the dogs've been poisoned, Trav."

"Who'd do a thing like that?" Les cried, rushing toward the stricken animals.

"Won't be hard to find out," Travis declared. "Sure to be fresh tracks nearby."

"Hard?" Les asked. "You won't find nothin' but tracks, Trav. Half the county was over here today, remember?"

"You can't be certain," Art said. "It was powerful hot. Maybe a coal got under the floorboards and—"

"Pa, a coal didn't steal that paper," Travis argued.

"I might've dropped it, son."

"You didn't drop it. It was took. And we all of us know who did it."

"Sam Delamer," Les said, tossing aside his spade and

glaring toward the river. "He's wanted us off this land. Well, he won't chase me off with a few flames."

"He doesn't have to," Travis said, picking up the spade. "He can close off the market road, ring this place with shot-guns, and force us to sell out or starve."

"He'll dam up the creeks first," Art said sorrowfully. "Like before. The well's near dry already, and our barrels are burned black as midnight."

"Les, get a wagon," Travis ordered. "Jesse, you go along."

"Where?" Les asked.

"Weatherford," Art said. "Gather up cloth, spices, flour, and beans."

"Rifles too," Travis added. "Plenty o' shells. Tinned food. Plenty o' shells, though, Les. Be a long autumn, and a longer winter. Lots o' Delamer hands, you know."

"I know," Les said. "Jess, come help ready the horses."

"I'll get our things organized," Edna volunteered.

"Bobby, Davy, you get along and help your sister," Art commanded. "Trav, let's have ourselves a walk, son."

The two older Cobbs stepped off a hundred yards or so before halting.

"You remember what we talked about before?" Art asked. "Sellin' out?"

"I remember, Pa."

"Be a good time. Nothin' good'll come o' this sort o' fight."

"I won't have my home stolen!" Travis cried. "Not this way! Pa, I been in hard fights before. Willie and me—"

"Willie's dead. And I'm old. All you got's your brothers and little Edna. I got no heart to see any of 'em killed, son."

"Nor do I," Travis said, gripping his father's gnarled hands. "But a man's got to stand up sometimes or he might as well crawl about like a worm. You want to teach Jess and Bobby and little Davy that the way to live's runnin' away when a wrong's done you?"

"You can't teach a dead boy nothin'."

"Leastwise he's not ashamed to speak his name. Sam Delamer's a long way from winnin' this fight. And he's not even begun to pay the price it'll cost!"

# CHAPTER 4

Sam Delamer watched with grim satisfaction the distant pillar of thick black smoke. It was strange the cleansing effect fire could have. The Comanches used to burn the prairie in order to bring on the spring grasses. When the old cabin down on the river had burned, hadn't the fine new house on the hill taken its place? **Well**, Sam thought, **I've burned out a blight on my dream. Now the Trident Ranch can grow anew.**

Matthew announced Chance Cooper's arrival an hour after dinner. Sam was treating himself to a short whiskey by way of reward, and he offered to pour the young gunman one as well.

"Thanks, Colonel," Cooper said, grinning as he drew from his pocket a crumpled sheet of paper. "This what you wanted?"

"The very thing," Sam said, exchanging a shot glass for the document. After reading it over, Sam carefully laid the paper in the fireplace and ignited it.

"Can't afford to have any proof, eh, Colonel?" Cooper asked.

"No, we wouldn't want anybody to think we had anything to do with the Cobbs' misfortune."

They shared a brief laugh. Then Sam drew out his cash box and provided young Cooper with the balance of his money.

"You know, Colonel, I was talkin' some with the boys," Cooper said as he pocketed the cash. "None of us much like the high-handed way them Cobbs been treatin' us. We thought you might like us to have a look at the way that creek flows onto their place."

"Oh, there's time for that," Sam said, pouring himself another whiskey. "They know it, too. Important thing to do is let 'em know how tight their position is."

"Block the road, you mean."

"Oh, I'd hate to have anybody think I'd cut off a neighbor from market," Sam said, nodding to himself. "But I have been meanin' to test that new wire James sent up from Austin."

"The barbed wire, you mean. Devil wire, they're callin' it. Some o' the folks down south are usin' it to cut up the open range."

"Fence off their grass so others don't abuse it. Makes sense, don't you think?"

"Be hard on the small folks."

"Those without river acreage," Sam said, running his finger along the map until it rested on the Cobb place. "Why not string that new wire, what we've got of it, along that southeast line."

"That'll cut the road, Colonel."

"Can't help that," Sam said, chuckling. "You wouldn't expect me to detour a fence all over the place, especially when it's on my land."

"Some might put up a gate."

"And trust their neighbors to keep it closed?" Sam asked, raising his eyebrows. "When it cuts their stock off from water? I look like a fool, young man?"

"No, sir," Cooper said, grinning. "I'll have the fellows get after it first thing tomorrow."

"You go along with 'em, Chance. Wouldn't want any harm to come of this."

"No harm to us, you mean," Cooper said, nodding as he turned to leave. "I hear you all right, Colonel. Trust me to see it's done."

Trust wasn't a thing Sam Delamer traded in. But he knew he could rely on greed and ambition to keep Chance Cooper at his work. Young Cooper also had a taste for murder, and a shot or two might hurry Arthur Cobb toward coming to terms.

Early that next morning Sam was out watching the wranglers work a pair of colts when Reverend John Wesley Ames, the Methodist circuit rider, appeared. J.W., as he was universally known, was near forty—old for the circuit, but he seemed to thrive on preaching hither and yon.

"Mornin', Sam," the preacher said, tipping his hat. "How are Helen and the new baby? I've missed you at meeting lately."

"Lots to do," Sam explained. "Helen's taking it rather easy for a time. Summer's hard on the gentler gender, you understand."

"I do indeed," Ames said, mopping his brow with a bandanna. "I fear August is a trial for us all. I do miss Helen's voice when it's time to sing the hymns, though."

"She misses the service herself," Sam assured the minister. "Did you come to look in on her?"

"Well, I'll take the opportunity to do that and to discuss the child's christening, but I mainly came to solicit the help of the community in assisting the Cobb family in their time of trial. You know, I gather, that there was a fire."

"Thought it possible. There was some smoke out that way. I sent riders," Sam added, "but they said the grass wasn't burning. I thought perhaps they were burning off brush."

"The house went, I'm afraid. Most of the furniture, some clothing . . ."

"I'll be more than willing to contribute, Reverend. Just let me go find my pocketbook."

"Actually, Sam, I was hoping you might provide something else."

"What would that be?" Sam asked.

"It seems a certain agreement was destroyed in the fire, a contract guaranteeing Art Cobb access to town via the market road we use now. It also assured him no dams would be built across the creeks."

"I don't know that I understand, Reverend."

"I was hoping you would let me draw up a similar document for you to sign. In that way everyone would be reassured the fire was an accident."

"I don't think I like the sound of that," Sam said, his face growing crimson. "You mean to imply I had something to do with that fire?"

"It's been said."

"Well, not to me, it hasn't. I'd be happy to trounce the man who's spreading such aspersions! As to this paper you speak of, there might have been something to that effect drawn up by my father. Or perhaps my brother William, when he was here, agreed to such terms. He was a good friend of Travis Cobb, you understand. But I have no knowledge of such a paper, and I'm not in the habit of pledging away sections of my property as right of way. Nor is the tragedy of a fire cause to force such an agreement from me, either. I don't like the tone of this whole conversation, and you can rest assured I'll be corresponding with the bishop in that regard."

"That's your privilege, Colonel, but I must tell you the bishop is well aware of sentiments in Palo Pinto County."

"He's also aware, sir, who's offered to build a church in town, who would provide the masons and the lumber, and who would pay the bulk of the operating funds once it was in place.''

''One man doesn't make a congregation, Sam.''

''No, but the right man's support can make or break you hereabouts, Reverend Ames. I've got close to fifty people working on this ranch, and close to a hundred others owe their living to us. I'd judge that the better part of the county's inhabitants, wouldn't you? So it could be I'm in a better position to speak for the people of Palo Pinto County than you are. Now I believe I'll bid you good day. I've got more important matters to turn my mind to.''

''You'll have no objection to my looking in on Helen and the baby?''

''At present, I don't consider you're particularly welcome on my land, Ames, and you certainly aren't free to spread your vile rumors to my poor wife. Can you leave on your own, or do you need an escort?''

''I know the way,'' the minister said, turning his horse and leaving immediately.

The wranglers exchanged grins, but Sam only muttered to himself. It was an ill wind indeed that blew the preacher into this business, and Sam thought it best to have a ride out to check on the fence crew.

There were few things in life as worrisome to Sam De-lamer as a ride on a horse. He loved to watch the creatures, from the quick-as-lightning cutting ponies to the sleekest thoroughbreds, but he'd never known comfort or balance in the saddle. Willie was the born horseman in the family, and young James rode with grace and polish, even if he didn't have the magic their brother possessed. For Sam, though, riding was agony.

He ordered a pair of stableboys to ready a carriage. The springs were none too sound, and the leather seat lacked a gentle nature. Still, being jostled about some wasn't half so deadly as blistered thighs, sore hip joints, and a twisted back would be.

He found Chance Cooper and a half-dozen men setting posts and stringing wire a quarter mile from where the Cobb ranch joined the Trident spread.

"You missed the boundary some," Sam told young Cooper.

"Know it, Colonel," Cooper answered. "Didn't figure it a good notion to be close enough to the boundary they could shoot at us or tear down the posts, sayin' they were on their land."

"I hadn't considered that," Sam said, nodding. Actually he would have welcomed such shooting. The Cobbs couldn't survive an out-and-out shooting war, and there wasn't anyone around to stop one.

Even as the ranch crew worked, a trio of riders approached on horseback. Sam recognized Arthur Cobb and his son Travis. The other horseman was one of the younger boys, perhaps Jesse. The younger Cobbs were all of a kind, strawberry blond and thin-faced like Ellen. Travis was darker, wound tight as a spring, and capable of considerable destruction. Willie's wartime letters from Virginia spoke of Travis as death on the wind. Nothing Sam noted hinted Travis had mellowed any.

"Seems you Delamers got yourself busy," Travis declared as he pulled his horse to a stop. "You wouldn't want to fence the road, though. We got a wagon comin' along soon, and we'd hate your work to go to waste."

"Meanin'?" Cooper asked.

"Wagon's got a right to pass down this road," Art answered. "We've got an agreement."

"Do we?" Sam asked. "I heard you had a fire, Art."

"Oh, we had a fire, all right," Travis said, frowning.

"And we know who started it," the younger brother cried. "You Delamers! Stole the paper and then burned down our house!"

The boy's hand touched the stock of a rifle, and Chance Cooper pulled his pistol and fired. The youngster howled as he clutched a shattered wrist, then slumped across his saddle as his father and brother fought to control their skittish horses.

"Bobby?" Travis called. "Bobby, you all right?"

"I just persuaded him to leave that rifle be," Cooper boasted. "If I'd wanted him dead, I'd planted him true enough."

"It's just my arm," the thirteen-year-old said, regaining his senses.

"It's none too good, Pa," Travis announced as he took a look. "Be best to bind it good, then get him along to Jack."

"Maybe you all should go," Sam said, grinning. "I've offered you fair money before, Art. I'll up it a hundred out of good faith."

"Nothin' good 'bout you, Sam Delamer," Art answered. "You sap the strength and vitality out of the land by over-grazin', then run your neighbors off to get their grass. You hire men your pa wouldn't spit on, and those who helped you, powdered your wet bottom when you weren't yet afoot, are treated like lepers. You eat your offer. We're here to stay!"

"Are you?" Sam asked. "We'll see."

Travis, who had been tearing his shirt into bandages, glanced back and glared. "Your man's gone and fired the first shot, Delamer!" he shouted. "It's war now."

"Has been a long time, Cobb," Sam answered. "Mind you stay on your side of the wire now, hear? Chance's got orders to shoot trespassers."

"Best he knows the difference 'tween a half-grown boy and Travis Cobb," Travis barked. "I'll be firin' back at anybody shoots in my direction. I've buried men before."

"So've I," Chance boasted. "Care to try your hand?"

"Oh, it may come to that. Just now I got a brother to tend. But by and by we'll get around to each and every one o' you. Even you, *Colonel* Sam."

Travis spoke the title with sarcasm and hate, bringing the crimson glow back to Sam's forehead. But before a reply could be managed, the Cobbs turned and rode back to their home.

"Make the fence strong," Sam urged. "And, Chance, keep somebody out here and where it crosses the creek. Those'd be the likely places they'll try to cut it."

"What about the wagon?" Cooper asked.

"Let it pass. You've given them enough to consider for one day. But from now on, nothing moves in or out. Understand?"

"I understand just fine, Colonel. We'll see to it. Don't you worry."

They did, indeed, blockade the Cobb ranch. The wire was cut now and then, and supplies were smuggled in, but the fence was having a telling effect. Young Bobby, together with Edna and Davy, passed the balance of August and the first week of September in Wise County with the Trents. Then, on September 10, the sky suddenly darkened, and the temperature dropped sharply.

"Get to cover!" Sam howled at his children as a dark rumbling sound shook the ground.

"It's like a train's goin' over us in heaven!" one of the stableboys cried.

"You'll be the one ends up in heaven if you don't get to shelter!" Sam howled. "Get low. It's a twister!"

Sam knew even before the funnel-shaped cloud dipped out of the ebony sky. There was a sensation you felt just before a tornado struck, and you didn't forget it easily. Twice before, Sam Delamer had witnessed the demon winds of a cyclone, but never had he known one to approach so close to his home and family.

He collected Helen and the children and forced them down into the root cellar. It was a dank, unpleasant place, and baby Stephen took to crying. Catherine nestled in under Sam's left arm, and little Sam whimpered as he clutched the right. Only Robert kept his distance. The eight-year-old seemed intent on guarding his mother and tiny brother.

The storm rumbled past overhead, ripping at roof shingles and uprooting trees. Glass shattered, and one wall was torn away. In the end, like all do, the storm passed, and the Delamers stumbled out of the cellar to a scene of utter confusion and disarray.

"Lord, what a mess," Helen said, sighing as she turned the baby over to Essie's eager hands.

"There's a hole in the roof," Catherine observed.

"Watch out for the glass," Sam advised. Then, as he stepped past a nasty shard, he saw a dark furry shape trapped by a roof beam.

"It's old Henry," little Sam said, hurrying toward the spot. "Poor dog."

"I should've gone looking for him," Robert declared. "He was a good dog. Once he killed a snake that was about to bite me. He got old, though, and he couldn't run very fast."

"Poor Henry," Catherine said, touching the bloody creature.

"He had a good life," Sam told the little ones. "And he didn't feel it."

"I'll miss him," Robert said, quivering.

"You all right, son?" Sam asked the boy.

"I won't cry, Papa," Robert pledged. "Delamers are hard, aren't they?"

"Yes, they are," Sam said, pulling back the hand he thought to offer.

"I'll bury him out back, if that's all right. He liked that spot."

"Get Matthew to help you," Sam suggested.

"No, I'll do it myself," Robert insisted. "He was my dog."

Sam watched Robert free the dog's corpse from the beam. Then, with rare tenderness, the boy carried the animal out through the gap in the back wall of the house.

Sam, meanwhile, sent a half-dozen hands to shore up the

walls and begin the repairs. He then set off to inspect the other damage.

The hay barn had lost a shutter, but the horse barn was unharmed. The animals and men seemed shaken, but that would pass. Sam was beginning to feel hopeful when a tattered Chance Cooper appeared.

"Lord, Colonel, you never seen anything like it," the young man declared. "Twister plunked herself down and just ate that ole fence like a mornin' biscuit. Tore out posts and everything! Tossed men and rocks 'round like they was nothin'! I got two o' my crew with stove-in ribs and another with a bad broke leg. We got horses down, and that dam we started on the creek's scattered all over everywhere."

"Best I go have a look," Sam said, turning back to get a carriage ready. But the carriage house was a shambles, and the horses were fractious. He ended up walking with Cooper to the road.

When they arrived, Arthur and Travis Cobb were tending the injured cowhands.

"Just about had us, eh, Sam?" Travis asked with a broad grin. "Laid siege to the place tighter'n Grant held Petersburg. Seems God had other notions, though. Shame 'bout your wire."

"There's more of it can be bought," Sam replied. "As to God, looks like I'll have to chat a bit with Him. He'll come around to my way of thinking."

"Or what? You won't build him a church?" Travis asked, laughing. "Even that Yank judge can't wrangle everything!"

Sam stared bitterly at his grinning neighbors and turned back toward the ranch. Even as he walked, he was preparing the telegrams that would bring the wire—and help.

# CHAPTER 5

Morgan Delaney appeared that same week. Tall and lean, with a big, drooping mustache that threatened to hide his chin, Delaney greeted each object in his view with a cold gaze. He did not bother making acquaintances. Instead he rode straight to the big house and passed word to Sam Delamer of his arrival.

"You had some trouble, it appears," Delaney said as he surveyed the tornado damage. "Somebody bring it down on you?"

"No, it was a storm," Sam explained. "Set our efforts back some, but it's nothing permanent."

"Ain't a thing on this earth is," Delaney said, tapping the ivory grips of his twin pistols.

"I sent for you because I plan to do some persuading soon. I have some neighbors who seem reluctant to sell their land."

"And I'll do the persuadin', eh?" Delaney asked. "You call the tune, Colonel Delamer. I'm up to what needs doin'. Pay'll be same as last time."

"Excellent. Why don't you have yourself a good wash, then settle in over at the bunkhouse. You know Chance Cooper. He'll fill you in on the details."

"Thought maybe you'd be doin' that yourself, Colonel," Delaney said, leaning against the door.

"I would, Morg, but I've got an appointment in Jacksboro I mustn't miss. Federal judge."

"Judge?" Delaney asked nervously.

"No worry for you, Morg. This one's on our side."

"Best way to have 'em, eh, Colonel?"

"Only way," Sam responded with a broad grin.

Shortly after dismissing Delaney, Sam climbed aboard a repaired carriage and nodded to Amos Burks, the young driver. Burks released the brake and slapped the horses into motion. The trip to Jacksboro was long and exhausting, especially via a dust-choked road in the early fall. Ordinarily Sam Delamer made the trip only once or twice a year, but a summons from DeWitt Fulton had come, and it wasn't altogether wise to spurn such an invite.

The journey took the better part of the day, though, and it was only after booking a room at Miss Beatrice McCall's boardinghouse and having a wash and a bit of dinner that Sam finally paid a call on Judge Fulton.

"Been expecting you," the judge said when his clerk, young Pat Tyler, escorted Sam into Fulton's sitting room. "Have a seat. We've got business to conduct."

"Surely, Judge," Sam said, grinning as he sat on a fine old divan no doubt liberated from some Southern aristocrat.

"I understand you've been paying a good deal of attention to the Cobb ranch of late," Fulton said. "Rather you not, Sam. Leave it for another time, old friend."

"Another time?" Sam asked. "That square of land sits plumb in the middle of my ranch. It's a sore spot rubbing me every minute."

"Still, I'd caution you against overextending yourself just now," Fulton warned. "Word has it the cattle market's in for a bad time, and taxes fall due in a month or so."

"You could help me out with the Cobbs, Judge," Sam said. "I don't figure old Art's got a real title to the place. He claimed it as part of his reward for service at San Jacinto, but I don't think he ever filed for a deed."

"I'll have Pat look into it. Any other properties you're interested in?"

"Then there's the Bayles place upriver. It's a fine spread, with a small flour mill and a peach orchard. They'll be pressed hard to pay their taxes, and I hear they're entertaining bids. You could check on their title, too. The mere word you're looking will drive the price down."

"I always said you were a good businessman, Sam."

"Man has to look for his opportunities, doesn't he, Judge? This occupation won't last forever."

"It feels as if it has already," Fulton grumbled. "It's those fools who haven't the sense to give up fighting us. There was a Negro senator attacked last week in Austin and nearly hung! Do you know there are people here in Jack County who've had the impudence to curse the very soldiers who are risking their lives to protect against Comanche and Kiowa incursions."

"There are hard feelings among some," Sam admitted. "That will pass, though."

"It had better, and soon, for their sakes. Elsewhere Rebels have been locked up for sedition."

"I don't think that will prove necessary here, nor in Palo Pinto County either. We've got a fair respect for the cavalry here and at Fort Griffin. Shoot, I'm due to sell them another fifty horses this month."

"Oh, as to that, there's been a change of mind. The cavalry's agreed to buy remounts from another party."

"But we had a contract," Sam protested. "I've had my people working those animals sunrise to sunset so they'd be ready."

"Pity, that."

"You and the post quartermaster both signed the agreement, Judge Fulton."

"As to the quartermaster, he's been transferred, I believe.

And do you really want to submit this matter to the court?'' the judge asked, raising an eyebrow.

"Little point to that," Sam muttered.

"I knew you'd see the light, Sam. Let me look into these title matters. And I wouldn't worry so much about that horse sale. Since you won't be buying the Cobb place, you should have plenty of cash to see you through the winter."

Sam gazed at the grin spreading across the Ohioan's face and sought to discover some hint of what might be going through the mind behind it. What was this new game Fulton was playing? Did he think he could walk away from agreements and thwart Sam Delamer's plans? That was a dangerous game indeed, even for a man backed by two companies of federal cavalry!

It was already late when Sam left the judge's quarters, but he headed straightaway to the telegraph office. The door was bolted, and the front office was closed, but Sam knew there would be a night operator manning the wire. The military required communications be open at all times.

"Hey, in there!" Sam called, rattling the door. "Open up."

This initial call brought no response, so Sam repeated it again and again. Finally, he tapped the windowpanes with his ring. The resulting sound was too annoying to long ignore, and the night operator finally appeared.

"We open at nine in the mornin'," a weathered old man with the stubby fingers of a telegraphist explained from the far side of the window. "Get along now, mister."

"You'll open that door or have cause to regret it," Sam said angrily. "Now!"

The operator stepped back as if to return to his post. Then, recognizing the determination in Sam's eye, he relented.

"Come along in," the old man grumbled as he unbolted the door. "It's late, you know. We don't keep night hours."

"You're up," Sam replied. "I've got a message needs to be in Austin tonight."

"Write it out. I'll get it sent."

"It's to be delivered immediately, and I'll expect you to get a reply to me over at Mrs. McCall's the instant it comes through."

"Lord, you'd guess I was talkin' to President Grant," the old-timer said. "I got no help to run wires to anybody. And—"

"I'll send a boy over to wait on the reply," Sam announced. "Now, let me get this written out or none of us is apt to get any rest this night."

"Yes, sir," the telegraphist said with a sigh.

Sam drafted the message cryptically, so as to prevent word galloping around town of his intentions. Telegraph offices were a sea of gossips in the daytime, both in Jacksboro and Austin. It was bad enough DeWitt Fulton knew so much of Sam's business. There was no point in letting everyone else in on it.

There were three telegrams in all. The first went to Sam's young brother James, inviting the young man to keep an ear open around the statehouse. The second went to Harold Easton, a sharp-eyed lawyer whose particular skill lay in land acquisitions. Easton was a true genius at disputing titles, and more than once he'd pried a considerable acreage from its rightful owners because the proper deeds and papers disappeared.

The final message flashed to Baldy Nichols, an Austin detective who had worked for Allan Pinkerton in Missouri and Kansas before heading south. Baldy called himself a "fixer." He put things right, and he didn't much care how he went about it. The summer before, a band of rustlers was preying on Palo Pinto cattle herds. Baldy appeared, and the thieving stopped. After a week nobody in the county rode the range after dark, in fact, and if a wayfaring cowboy or two got himself shot by accident, well, life had its risks, didn't it?

While Easton was to investigate the background of the

Cobb and Bayles holdings, Baldy Nichols was to check on the dealings of one DeWitt Fulton.

"Best know your enemies," Big Bill Delamer had taught his son. **Best know your friends even better,** Sam thought.

After writing the messages and watching the telegraphist transmit them, Sam headed along to Mrs. McCall's place. The spry widow had, in addition to her boarders, five children of her own and a pair of nephews to look after, and Sam had no trouble finding a shaggy-haired boy named Raleigh eager to earn half a dollar by running the answers to the telegrams over.

"Bring them as soon as they arrive," Sam told the boy. "No matter how late or how early. Knock on the door, then come on in. I need them yesterday."

"I'll get four bits for each, Mr. Delamer?"

"So long as they get up here before breakfast."

"They'll be here. For a dollar and a half I'd run to Austin and bring 'em up myself!"

Sam laughed as the unkempt youngster sped out the door and over to the telegraph office. War had been hard on widows and orphans, but it made for a handy source of cheap labor. Good for business. Sam's kind anyway.

It proved to be a restless night for Sam Delamer. Much was on his mind, and he had trouble setting it aside long enough to sleep. Even when he did close his eyes, he found his dreams troubled by phantoms. Willie was there, laughing as he swaggered around the ranch, finding fault with this and that.

Fulton was there, too. His icy gaze was more chilling than Willie's threatening fingers on the grip of a pistol. But before much could happen, there was Raleigh McCall, shaking Sam awake in order to pass along a telegram.

From James and Baldy Nichols came similar answers.

"UNDERSTAND MESSAGE. WILL ATTEND TO MATTER."

Lawyer Easton promised to send papers on the midweek stage. It would, after all, take a day at least to track down all

the deeds and title papers, especially since Art Cobb's holdings involved a veteran's allotment.

"Takes time," Easton had said. "Have patience."

Time? Patience? Sam Delamer had neither.

It was a monumental trial for Sam to stay in Jacksboro
those next two days, awaiting news that was unlikely to offer
much promise. If there had been a soul in town to trust with
Easton's papers, Sam would have hired them delivered. But
Judge Fulton had long arms, and it would be tempting fate
to trust anyone to elude those arms.

When the papers did arrive, Sam took them to his room
at Mrs. McCall's and read them carefully. There wasn't an
ounce of good news to be found therein. In point of fact, it
was worse than might have been imagined.

To begin with, the Bayles place had been sold to agents
representing some Northern buyer. Easton discovered the
buyers received a large sum the day before from Jacksboro,
though. From whom? Judge DeWitt Fulton.

"Lord, he's turned my own game against me!" Sam
shouted as he crumpled the pages in his hand. He smoothed
them out again, however, for there was more. Art Cobb's
deeds were in good order. The statehouse clerks knew, for
someone else had recently sought that information.

"Fulton!" Sam cried, slamming his hand down on the
pine desk as fury spread through his chest. "He's buying up
land . . . likely with my own tax money!"

Another time Sam would have thought things out, considered ways of striking back. But emotion set his feet in motion, carried him along to the courthouse, and sent him
marching past young Pat Tyler and on into Fulton's private
chambers. Sam slammed the door shut and stormed over to
where the judge sat gazing at a stack of papers on his desk.

"Sam, a gentleman knocks before entering a room," Fulton chided.

"Don't you lecture me on manners, you Ohio snake!"
Sam answered. "All this time you've been asking my help,

securing my support, while all the while you intended to stab me in the back.''

"Oh, I wouldn't choose that metaphor, Sam. After all, I didn't starve my neighbors off their land. I didn't dispute the titles of men my own father called friend. No, I never claimed saintly motives, did I?''

"You knew I had the Bayles place in my plans,'' Sam pointed out.

"So did I. You expect me to be as free in announcing my strategy as you were? I'm not near such a fool.''

"And I suppose your warning about the Cobb place was to keep my hands off so you could buy it yourself.''

"Perhaps, given time,'' Fulton said with a sneer. "At present it's not worth a lot. You control the surrounding acreage, after all. But we've recently drawn up plans for a market road and a bridge over the river. That road would pass near the present trail the Cobbs use for trips to town, and I see no reason not to lengthen it and put up the bridge.''

"Costs money, building bridges,'' Sam said, eyeing the grinning judge with apprehension. "You wouldn't have a lot of reserve after buying the Bayles place.''

"That's true, Sam. Clearly the county will need another levy. Bridge tax.''

"For a bridge over the Brazos?'' Sam asked. "A bridge over a river that's got two dozen fords along that stretch?''

"Well, maybe we'll erect the bridge elsewhere, perhaps on the market road to Weatherford.''

"That's not in Palo Pinto County,'' Sam argued. "And there's a ferry there.''

"Oh, ferries can get very expensive. As to locations, the quality of the surveys we get now is simply terrible.''

"You're a liar and a thief, Fulton!''

"Take care of your speech, Sam,'' the judge said, laughing to himself. "A more sensitive person than myself might charge that contempt, even sedition. A bit of jail time might salve your feelings.''

"You're not that stupid."

"Oh, you can rest assured of that, Sam. I've never been accused of that sin. You've thrown a lot of words around today. Now hear me. I won't tolerate such a scene as this again. It's time you saw the true picture of things. Life as you've known it, before the war and after, is at an end. You'll survive only so long as I choose to have it so. Understand? I may have need of you. Pray I do. If not, you might be interested to know I had Pat investigate the titles of all Palo Pinto County landholders. It appears Arthur Cobb's papers are in considerably better order than your own."

"What?" Sam cried.

"I found no listing of a Delamer among the San Jacinto rosters. Nor was Pat able to find any land grants."

"You're crazy, Fulton. Bill Delamer and his father both got land for their service in the revolution. My father also fought the Mexicans down in the Neuces strip in the early forties and was a full major during the Mexican War. Afterward he fought the Comanches. He received grants each time."

"I don't doubt a word of it, Sam. Clearly the records seem to have been lost," the judge said, feigning sympathy. "Proof, on the other hand, is another matter. There've been a lot of titles and related papers destroyed by fire lately, you know."

Sam's eyes burned as he glared at the Ohioan.

"I've got copies of every scrap of paper ever given to Papa regarding the ranch," Sam declared. "Additional documents have been entrusted to attorneys in Austin and New Orleans. I may not have been cautious in placing trust in you, but I'm not fool enough to have my papers resting in a desk drawer where any passerby could help himself to them."

"You've been prudent to do so, Sam. Now all you have to do is keep up the taxes and make a money crop or two. That shouldn't be hard if the markets hold. Of course, if they should happen to falter . . ."

"You'd be there to see the ranch wouldn't fall into the hands of a stranger, wouldn't you?"

"Now see how clever you can be when you choose?"

"This isn't over, Fulton. Not by a long shot. We've got dealings yet ahead of us, and you'll come to regret tangling with me."

"That a threat, Sam?" the judge asked.

"Take it as you wish," Sam answered as he turned to go.

"You'll find the U.S. government doesn't take well to threats! You could find yourself in prison."

"That right?" Sam asked, pausing as he opened the door. "Worse things can happen to a man out here. Be careful where you ride, Judge Fulton. Not much moonlight just now. We've had road agents about before. They could come back. Sure could."

Sam didn't wait for a reply. Instead he slammed the door, strode past Pat Tyler, and continued along outside. He was anxious to get to the stable and have the carriage made ready. The ranch was a long way away just now. And Sam had never been as eager to return there.

# CHAPTER 6

In the days that followed, things didn't get any easier for Sam Delamer. If anything, life grew even harder. To begin with, Helen's brother Clayton Stanpole bombarded Sam with telegrams, pleading for a loan to salvage his failing business.

"Can't you provide the loan?" Helen asked when the next telegram came to her instead. "Three thousand dollars. Is it so much?"

"More than I have," Sam said, sighing. "We've sent money to Clayton before, dear, and what's come of it? I carry six thousand currently owed, plus interest. We'll never see a dime of it. New Orleans isn't a place for an enterprising Southerner to thrive any more than Palo Pinto is."

"Is it that bleak?" she asked.

"Worse. It appears Judge Fulton has set his sights on the Trident. We'll begin to feel some heavy pressure soon."

"Sam?"

"I've sent word to Harold Easton, and to James as well. They're doing what they can in Austin, but in the end it won't amount to a whole lot. I espect us to suffer some."

"Perhaps there's someone you know who would provide Clayton his loan."

"Helen, write your brother. Tell him I can't help, nor is there anyone south of Philadelphia who can. But if he's in need of a position, I'm sure we can find a place for him on the ranch. He used to have a good head for figures."

"Papa always thought so, as did the deans at William and Mary."

"Extend my sympathies and explain our own needs. Then invite him to join our struggle."

"I'll do so gladly. It will be good to see something of my family. Perhaps he'll make it by Christmas," Helen said, smiling. "We should perhaps plan a family gathering. We can write to Mary in Colorado, and—"

"She's got her own family now," Sam argued. "James will come home. That will be enough family."

Helen knew better than to argue the point. Sam had put on his grim, hard-jawed frown, the one from which he never backed down.

Autumn that year proved a trial at the Trident Ranch. At the same time as beef and remount contracts with the army were being voided right and left, DeWitt Fulton developed some new tax scheme each week.

"Another bridge tax?" Sam asked when a youthful blue-coat lieutenant arrived at the ranch in October. "We've paid for two bridges already, and we haven't seen a single plank laid yet!"

"You Rebs ought not to argue," the lieutenant warned. "There's been men thrown into jail for inciting rebellion in Texas."

Sam swallowed his anger and struggled to accept each new oppression as it came. The presidential election campaign was in full swing, and there was wide talk of electing the moderate Horatio Seymour and putting aside President Johnson's reconstruction programs.

It wasn't to be. The day Sam showed up to cast his own ballot, he was met by a squad of Negro policemen who announced Judge Fulton had failed to certify two-thirds of the voters in Palo Pinto County.

"He can't do that," Sam argued. "I signed the loyalty pledge."

"He can do what he want," a tall, broad-shouldered policeman announced. "We ain't goin' to let you Rebs cheat us of our rights no more."

So it was in Palo Pinto County that only two dozen freedmen and a few "reconstructed" whites—namely those expressing Republican views, cast ballots. There was, in addition, talk of wagons full of former slaves being taken from one county to another in order to assure the Republican candidates of victory. No one was much surprised when the newspapers related the election of the Northern hero, U. S. Grant, as new president.

"Grant the drunkard, we call him in New Orleans," Clayton Stanpole explained upon his arrival. "He's just a name for the radicals to hide behind. The great hero! Now the South will really see suffering."

Such grim election news hung heavily over the Trident Ranch that cold, snowy Christmas of '68. The ranch's dwindling cash reserves were especially felt, for a third of the bunkhouse berths were unoccupied, and the children had to be content with odds and ends, handed-down clothes and new shoes mainly.

It grated on Sam to learn of the fine party DeWitt Fulton held for his political friends in Jacksboro the first of January. Once Sam would have been invited. Now he had become the prime victim. Each time a levy was made against the county, the Trident Ranch's share grew in proportion. Moreover, Fulton's market road defeated Sam's every effort to strangle the Cobb place into submission.

The worst still lay ahead, though. A hard winter had thinned out the cattle herd, but spring birthings hit a new high. Ten spry new colts raced each other around the horse corral, too. And a considerable band of mustangs had been chased down near the river and brought in for breaking.

Of all the animals, the most handsome was a bay mare. That horse had strength and heart. In addition, she was gentle and steady the way a good saddle horse should be. Young Robert was particularly drawn to the animal, and the stable hands had to pry the boy off the horse to get him to dinner on time.

"I got a birthday coming, Papa," Robert hinted time and again. "Seems to me a man needs a good horse if he's going to call himself a Texan."

"A good horse?" Sam asked, feigning ignorance of the matter.

"Take that bay. She's the kind of horse a man half-grown could ride hard and never have to worry."

"A half-grown man?" Sam asked. "Who'd that be?"

"Me!" Robert cried. "I'll be nine, Papa. Uncle Jamie was grown at sixteen, wasn't he? I'm more than halfway there, don't you see?"

"And you want that bay?"

"More than anything," Robert confessed. "I'd tend her proper, Papa. I've learned how to comb the burrs out of her hair, and I'm tending her already, bringing oats and water."

"And you feel the bay's the one you want?"

"I love her, Papa. It means a lot."

"Then on your birthday, she's yours," Sam promised.

But before the day dawned, Fulton's arrogant young lieutenant arrived with a handful of papers.

"What's this about a tax seizure?" Sam asked angrily as he scanned the papers. "I've paid my bills."

"This isn't a new tax exactly," the lieutenant explained. "It's just, well, we had a fire in Jacksboro, and some of the military supplies burned. There are needs, and we've come to satisfy them."

"You plan to pay for all this then?"

"If we did, the judge would simply have to increase the

taxes to cover the expense. Makes more sense to draw up a list and take what we need."

"Not to me," Sam argued. "This isn't legal. You can't simply take my property without a hearing!"

"Oh, I think we can," the lieutenant said, grinning. "We're doing just that. If you've got a complaint, address it to Judge Fulton."

"I'll address it to others as well," Sam replied angrily. "Even the scalawags in Austin and Washington won't sanction out-and-out theft!"

"I'd remind you that you are addressing a federal officer!" a corporal barked. "Lieutenant Merritt, you want maybe I should throw a rope 'round him so we can drag him along back to Jacksboro?"

"I wouldn't think too hard on that," Morgan Delaney said, stepping out of the bunkhouse. Three or four other hands, including Chance Cooper, appeared in windows cradling rifles, and the corporal backed away.

"Gather the supplies!" Merritt commanded. "Especially the oats."

"We need those oats for the horses," a young stableboy named Ollie Griffin complained. A bluecoat slung the youngster out of the way and went on seizing the neatly stacked sacks of feed from the barn.

"You won't need these," a scowling sergeant announced. "We've got need of horses, too."

Sam clawed at a fence rail as the bluecoats raided the ranch of its best animals.

"Them soldiers'll break 'em down in a month's service," young Griffin grumbled. "If the Comanches don't steal 'em first."

"Ought to let the colonel keep the horses and give us leave to go after them Indians!" Delaney suggested. "We know how to put a stitch in their gullets, don't we?"

The other hands laughed, and half a smile came to Sam's

lips. It faded as Lieutenant Merritt led the bay mare out of the ready corral.

"No, you can't!" Robert screamed as he raced toward the horse. The animal reared up at Robert's approach and kicked the lieutenant in the side. The officer rolled over toward the fence and barely avoided being trampled. Other hands quickly took charge of the bay.

"She's mine!" Robert said as he hugged the horse's proud neck. "Papa promised her to me on my birthday."

"You remember how it was with your first horse, Lieutenant," Cooper said, nodding toward the boy. "He's been out here workin' the mare day and night. There's others as good."

"Consider it a favor done me," Sam said, helping Merritt to his feet. "I pay a fair return for services done me."

"You're not in a position to make promises *or* ask favors!" Merritt barked. "Take the horse, Corporal, and let's get along. We've other visits to make this day."

"Papa!" Robert shouted as a pair of soldiers pried him from the mare.

"Let the boy be!" Delaney warned.

"Put your guns away, boys," Sam said, staring at the anger silently exchanged between the cowhands and the soldiers. "This isn't our day."

"There's things worth fightin' for," Cooper argued.

"And dying for, too, but this isn't one of them," Sam declared. "I've buried one boy. I wouldn't want to lose a second on account of a horse."

"But it's not just a horse, Papa," Robert said, hurrying to his father's side. "She's special."

"Not special enough to start a war over, son," Sam asserted. "Now get along inside and dust yourself off. We'll find you another horse."

"I don't want another one," Robert said, staring bitterly at both his father and the bluecoats. "Not ever."

"You'll change your mind once the sting wears off," Sam argued.

"It won't wear off, Papa. How long will you let 'em do this to us?"

Sam read the disappointment in his eldest son's face, and it humbled him. For the first time in ages, he reached out a hand to comfort the boy. Robert stepped back to avoid Sam's touch.

"Won't be forever, Robert," Sam promised. "Our day will come, and there's one young soldier who will be dearly sorry for the mistake he just made."

The confiscations of property and supplies at the area ranches raised a great outcry. For once Sam sensed a common grievance, and he wasted no time inviting his neighbors for a county meeting. More than half actually came. Among them were Art and Travis Cobb.

Sam Delamer hadn't spoken with the Cobbs since the storm. He'd sent regrets about the "misunderstanding" several times since Christmas, but there had been no reply. At the monthly camp meetings held by Reverend Ames down at the river, Helen brought baskets of fruit for the neighbors, but most were refused.

"Don't need such as I can't provide myself," Homer Shetland declared. Most of the others felt similarly. The Cobbs merely turned away angrily—especially young Bobby, who rubbed his scarred arm and glared.

"I brought you all here to discuss our common trouble," Sam told the assembled farmers and ranchers. "These confiscations have to end! It's little more than wholesale banditry!"

The crowd muttered its agreement, but Travis Cobb answered less agreeably.

"Suddenly grown concerned for the neighbors, Sam?" Travis asked. "Weren't much bothered when it was just others that judge was robbin'."

"It's never been only one of us that's suffered," Sam argued. "When Comanches swept across this valley, threatening to kill every white man in sight, who rallied the people and led the fight? Bill Delamer. When the men set off to fight the Mexicans and later the Unionist invaders, who stood at the head of the column? Bill Delamer. And who was it avenged those dreadful Kiowa and Comanche raids that filled so many graveyards back in sixty-four? Wasn't it myself?"

"Fine thing that was, slaughterin' a bunch o' womenfolks and little kids," Shetland replied. "The men went up to Young County and rode through the ranches there like a whirlwind. Some of us went up to help 'em. Wasn't you led *them*, Sam!"

"You're no Big Bill Delamer," Art Cobb added. "Nor even the man your brother Willie was. Was him fought the real Comanches."

"It's time we put aside our differences," Sam argued. "It's either band together or perish separately."

"If you go, too, Sam, I'm not so certain I'd altogether mind," Art replied, laughing.

"There's no humor to our plight," Sam declared.

"I for one am tired o' sheddin' blood to solve your problems, Sam Delamer," Shetland said. "My boy George followed you into Arkansas. While you was runnin' for high grass at Elkhorn Tavern, he stood fast and got himself gutshot. Now he's buried up in Arkansas, far from home and loved ones. Then there was Jerome. Lost a leg trailin' your cows to Kansas, he did, but you paid him half wages on account you had to leave him south o' Wichita with a rustler's ball in his knee."

"I got him top price for his steers, though."

"You got a powerful conscience where money's concerned, Sam!" Shetland hollered. "But we stand by you and deal with these Yanks, how long afterward will our houses burn? When'll you dam up our creeks?"

"You go your own way, there'll be no need," Sam argued.

"Judge Fulton'll own every stick in this county by summer's end. Would you rather those Northern devils steal you blind than help a Southerner and a neighbor?"

"Guess you're a Southerner, but I wouldn't call you a neighbor," Shetland answered.

"As for devils," Travis added, "they seem to grow tall both sides o' the Mason–Dixon line."

The crowd stirred angrily, and Sam stood defenseless as one remembered outrage after another was related. In the end the others went home in smug satisfaction, leaving Sam to stare at their departing dust.

"They won't be much help, Colonel," Morgan Delaney observed.

"I gave them their chance," Sam growled. "Now we'll tend our own business and leave them to their own fate!"

# CHAPTER 7

Sam Delamer tried a dozen enticements to gain the support of his neighbors, but memories along the Brazos were long, and the other ranchers were powerfully short of trust. Up-river, the Bayles place and two other ranches besides were gobbled up by DeWitt Fulton's Brazos River Combine—a group of businessmen, ranchers, and politicians with the common goal of making a fortune in a hurry. Sam could only watch with begrudging admiration the way the judge snapped up one holding after another.

"The money and the law," Clayton Stanpole remarked. "That's a pair wins every hand."

Morgan Delaney and Chance Cooper thought otherwise.

"Give us leave, Colonel," young Chance pleaded. "I'll drop that Yank crook quick and sure. Then he'll trouble no-body!"

"Get us all hung in the bargain," Delaney argued. "We're the first ones the cavalry'd come to, ain't we, Colonel?"

"I'd leave no proof," Cooper explained. "They'd never tie any of us to it."

"When a man writes his own laws, he don't need proof," Delaney answered.

61

"He's right, you know," Sam agreed. "No, only way to shave Fulton's to hang him on his own gallows. And that'll take some real doing. You boys just keep your eyes open. Something will come along we can use to loosen his grip hereabouts."

But as days became weeks, and the first sunrise of summer arrived, no method of escaping the judge's tight grip appeared. Fulton's taxes had nearly emptied Sam's cash accounts at the banks in Jacksboro and Austin. Moreover, the cruel confiscations cut into food supplies and livestock herds.

"We've had such lean times before," Sam told his roundup crews as they labored to collect the cattle for the yearly counting. "It's said the markets are bad just now, but Texas beef always brings a fine price at the Kansas railheads. What's more, if we get there early, there will be a bonus to every man who comes along."

"Colonel, there's a lot o' hirin' goin' on just now," a dour-faced cowboy named Bobby McDowell pointed out. "Man can always find a job in the summer. Some of us nigh starved last winter, though. I'd rather have your promise of a winter berth in the bunkhouse than fifty dollars bonus money."

"How would you feel about a hundred?" Sam asked. "As to winter, I've always kept as close to a full crew as I could afford. It would be no favor to keep men I couldn't pay."

"I'd work for food and shelter," McDowell argued. "How 'bout the rest o' you?"

Several of the younger hands nodded their agreement, and Sam scowled. He resented being cornered into making promises. But only a fool ran men off at roundup time, especially when other ranches a half day's ride away, were hiring.

"I never sent a cowboy from my table anytime," Sam declared. "Even those working elsewhere know the Trident's good for a plate of beef and beans. Of course, if we fail to get a fair price for our steers, we may all be looking for a place to sling our hats come December.''

The others laughed at the thought of Sam Delamer set adrift. Sam didn't share their grins. He felt DeWitt Fulton's fingers closing in on him, tightening their grip on his throat.

As the crew continued the exhausting task of collecting the cattle, branding the yearlings, and gelding nine of ten bull calves, Sam rode through the county, doing his best to muster help from the neighboring ranches.

''We've always combined our interests on the long drives to Kansas,'' Sam said again and again. ''We'll take along your cattle for the help your hands can provide.''

''Sure, we remember it all too well,'' young Herbert Finch replied. ''Pa trusted you back in sixty-six when we went to Wichita, and we had a fair accountin' then 'cause your brother took charge. But in sixty-seven and again last summer, our cows mostly got lost along the way, and you paid my brother Billy and me together less'n one o' your hands took home. We started with fifty steers, you know. Got paid for four delivered.''

''You might have done a better job looking after them,'' Sam scolded. ''The two of you were young, though.''

''Won't wash, Mr. Delamer. I saw better'n forty o' our beeves to the Arkansas River. Couldn't so many wander from there onto the Wichita pens. Pa's dead, and there's ten o' us to feed and clothe on this place. We'd all o' us starved if Trav Cobb hadn't offered us help. Billy and me'll be headin' out with Trav's bunch this time.''

''He'll not get the price I secure from those Kansas City buyers!'' Sam warned.

''Maybe not, but we'll be sure to get our rightful cut. And Trav's already got most o' the herd gathered south o' the Clear Fork, ready to head out with Mr. Ted Slocum.''

''Slocum!'' Sam stormed. So that was it! Travis had drawn the others in with his old war buddy Slocum. They'd have enough of a crew to leave the Trident to struggle north on its own.

"You watch yourself on the trail north, youngster," Sam said, shaking his head as he turned to leave. "You're sure to run across trouble going with those two."

"Not so much as you'll find without 'em, I'll vow," Herb declared. "Likely we'll see you 'long the way, Mr. Delamer. Or on our way home more likely."

Sam stared angrily at the cocky young man. A year ago Chance Cooper would have paid those Finches a visit. Now, well, there was just too much to do.

The Finches weren't the only Palo Pinto ranchers throwing in with the Cobbs and Ted Slocum. Slocum had built a sprawling ranch out on the Clear Fork of the Brazos, and his herds increased beyond all reason. Even as hunters from The Flat thinned the dwindling buffalo herds, longhorns spread across the broad llano to eat the buffalo grass.

"I could bring in fifty thousand head with a big enough crew," Slocum boasted. "Enough beef to feed the country!"

"And drive the price down to a stump," Travis argued. "Three thousand's as big a herd as can be managed across the Nations, Ted, and that'll bring you a nice profit, especially if we get there early."

"Always do, Trav," Slocum pointed out. "I put those Mexican boys to work with the extra horses, and except for your four hundred and what's left on the ranches across the Brazos, the herd's ready to go. You name the day, and we're off."

"Day after tomorrow," Travis declared. "It'll take one day to wind our steers along that fool market road, and another to head 'em along to the Clear Fork."

"If the rivers don't flood, we'll be one o' the early outfits to hit Wichita."

"Don't have to be first," Travis asserted. "Just have to beat Sam Delamer in."

"That's gone and gotten awful personal, hasn't it?" Slocum asked. "Hard to believe you'd ever come to such hard feelin's concernin' the major's own brother."

"The major?" Travis asked sourly. "You forget Abilene, how Sam hired that fellow Johnson to shoot Willie? His own brother! It's why Willie didn't come back, why he's wandered off into the mountains. Most likely got himself shot or starved on some hilltop, colder'n the Petersburg line even."

"Ain't nothin' colder'n that," Slocum grumbled.

"Leastwise there were friends there," Travis argued. "And a hair o' hope."

Sam Delamer saw the dust clouds raised by the Cobb cattle and the smaller ones stirred up by the Finches and other neighbors. Never had Sam felt so beset by circumstance. The weight of the world pressed down on him, and there were no allies to share his gloom.

"How far are we from getting the herd in order?" Sam asked the crew heads. "A day or so? A week?"

"Be three weeks to a month to do it proper," old Shag Mapps suggested. "We could get a thousand head started, then bring the rest along. Maybe Slocum's bunch would let you tie up with 'em."

Sam didn't bother responding. His fiery eyes silenced Mapps, and a moment later he dispatched Chance Cooper and Morg Delaney to instruct the cowboys a trail herd was to be gathered by sundown tomorrow.

"As for the branding and gelding, Mapps and the stable-boys can attend to it," Sam announced. "Ought to keep you busy till we get back."

"Keep us busy to Christmas, more likely," Mapps grumbled.

Sam didn't respond. Mapps had earned a discharge, but for the moment he would serve a purpose. Once the others were back, the old-timer could be sent packing. For now leaving him with a gaggle of young Negroes sure to shy from the task at hand was fitting reprisal.

Sam spent his final day making his good-byes. He left his brother-in-law to tend the day-to-day workings of the ranch until the trail crew's return. Except for the cash deemed necessary for the expenses of the crossing to Kansas, Sam left all the money in Clayton Stanpole's charge.

"Be frugal," he warned the younger man. "Keep a reserve back against any new tax bill Fulton delivers. And keep a man on guard at night. Back in sixty-eight we had some Comanches come through when the crew left."

"I'll see everything's tended," Stanpole promised. "As for a guard, young Chance left me his cousin Matt."

Sam nodded. Matt Cooper couldn't have been much older than sixteen, but he had the dark eye of a killer. In the end, that and the willingness to shoot mattered more than years.

Normally the Trident Ranch assembled as many as five thousand steers for the hard drive to Wichita. But with a small crew of twelve men and a half-dozen boys recruited from among the orphans at Weatherford and Jacksboro, Sam reluctantly agreed to leave all but two thousand head to enjoy another year's grazing. A cook was found at The Flat, as were a pair of renegades Chance Cooper suggested would prove of help if trouble appeared.

It was an outfit weak on experience and short on discipline. A good foreman might have welded them together, but Sam gave Morg Delaney the job, and Delaney lacked the patience to mold good cowboys from the desperate children that made up a third of the crew. The dozen good ones soon went in want of sleep, for the youngsters were next to useless after dark. What was worse, the point cowboys never kept the cattle moving straight, and many a mile was wasted wandering northward.

The first real trouble came when the Trident herd reached Red River Station. The best crossings were already crowded with longhorns, and a Chickasaw Indian guide named Joseph Iron Hawk directed Sam to a little-used ford to the east.

"Keep cows straight line," the Indian warned. "Sinking sand everywhere. Sinking sand!"

"Quicksand?" Sam asked.

Iron Hawk nodded.

Sometimes the entire Red River seemed to be one long bed of quicksand, but a good crew could keep its stock moving fast enough to avoid the treacherous bogs. Even a brief holdup, though, would cause the loss of fifty, even a hundred animals. Sam briefed his men on the dangers, and he personally assigned the best men the task of channeling the steers into a swift-moving line. But once the first cattle surged into the river, bawling and crowding together in a solid sea of hooves and horns, there was no hope of maintaining control. Thirsty animals paused to drink, and the first few became trapped by the quicksand.

"Throw a rope over their heads and drag 'em along!" young McDowell shouted. "Don't let 'em get to your horse, boy!"

One of the Jacksboro youngsters did just that. A horn punctured a pinto's lung, and the horse whinnied as it died in midstream.

"Help!" the boy cried. "Cain't swim!"

Another of the orphans hurried to his friend's aid, leaving the whole right flank open. It was in that very direction that the longhorns surged. Frightened by the whining horse and the terrified howls of the unhorsed cowboy, the animals swam through the river and raced on over the banks and into the wilds beyond.

"Hold those animals!" Sam hollered from his perch atop the cook wagon. "Cut them off!"

But there was no one to do it. The whole herd stampeded one way or another, with at least a third of the fool steers bolting south into the maze of ravines and brush-strewn creeks that led to the Trinity bottoms.

Worse lay ahead. Cowboys screamed as the charging cattle overran them. Boys waved hats or slapped rope ends at the beasts, but all to no avail. Half the outfit struggled to avoid drowning while others dragged themselves ashore, screaming in agony from where horns had laid open legs or splintered bones.

Then, as Sam shook his head in dismay, Morgan Delaney made a final effort to turn the herd. He fired his pistol into the air, and two hundred steers were suddenly storming back toward the river. At that moment Sam Delamer was pulling a half-grown cowboy onto the wagon while A. C. Dimmett, the cook, kept the mules plodding along through the mucky river bottom.

"Lord, no!" the soggy boy exclaimed when he caught sight of the cattle now bolting toward the helpless wagon. The cook couldn't turn the muddy wheels. He had no choice but to continue onward, hoping the cattle might ignore the wagon. But frothing with fury and beyond panic, the cattle simply continued oblivious to anything in their way.

*"Hee yoo!"* a deep voice then bellowed, and seven riders charged along the river's north bank and cut the cattle off from the bank. Cowboys, helplessly looking on as death hurled down atop them, raised a cheer for their rescuers.

"Lord, I thank 'ee," the boy beside Sam cried as he shivered in his wet shirt and trousers. "Ma was right, Colonel. Helps to pray!"

"More likely he hated to see the devil get so many good sinners so early in the day," A. C. Dimmett declared.

Sam's attention was elsewhere, though. He gazed first at the derelict hands that were being pulled out of the river, then at the scattered cattle, and finally at the grim face of his savior.

"Seems you found some trouble, Sam," Travis Cobb declared as he slapped dust from his hat. "Best crossin's upstream a ways."

"Seemed to be occupied," Sam grumbled.

"Well, sometimes it's time well spent waitin' on another outfit to cross," Travis pointed out. "Lot o' work you got yourselves, roundin' up your herd."

"I suppose you'd best leave us to it, too," Sam responded angrily.

"Thanks for cuttin' them cows off, mister," Bobby McDowell said as he discarded his saturated clothes. "Saved us proper."

"Sure did!" the others echoed. As they raised another cheer Travis stared into the hostile eyes of Sam Delamer.

"Call it a favor returned," Travis said, frowning. "For an old friend's sake. Don't go expectin' another, either."

"Didn't ask for this one!" Sam barked.

"Should've let you drown," Travis said, shaking his head. "Was a mistake Willie made once, savin' your hide. Likely I'll regret it, too."

**Could be,** Sam thought as he watched Travis lead the other rescuers westward along the river. But that moment he had a bigger worry. Thousands of Trident steers were scattered hither and yon, and all he had for a roundup crew were a bunch of half-trampled cowboys and petrified boys.

# CHAPTER 8

Ψ

It took half a week to reassemble something of a herd from the wild, ravine-scarred barrens north and south of the Red River. Even with small clusters of steers driven over by other trail crews, Sam only collected eight or nine hundred animals. Another hundred or so were gathered in by a small band of Chickasaws. Sam recognized Joseph Iron Hawk among them, and he approached the scout red-faced with anger.

"So, that was your game, was it?" Sam called. "Lead a man's cattle into a bog and steal him blind!"

"Ah, we've learned many tricks from the white man," Iron Hawk answered. "He's a good thief!"

The Indians howled with disdain before driving the cattle off to the north. Sam, with only five or six men fit to ride, was in no position to pursue.

"Chance and I could follow 'em, teach 'em some manners," Delaney offered. "Be a time rememberin' the Trident brand."

"You could kill some of them," Sam agreed. "But we have to cross this stretch of country every year, and I'd rather

70

not fight the Chickasaws every season. Besides, we couldn't handle two thousand steers now anyway.''

Delaney followed Sam's gaze toward the makeshift camp where A. C. Dimmett doctored cowboys. Already four of the hands had been taken to Red River Station. With broken hips or stove-in ribs, they'd never make the trip. As it was, two of the trail veterans rode the flanks with splinted legs, and a third carried his right arm in a sling. Three less fortunate others, including two of the boys signed on in Weatherford, were buried beneath a tall willow overlooking the fateful crossing.

''We're a week late startin', shy half the herd, and lackin' a dozen drovers,'' Bobby McDowell observed. ''Fine beginnin', eh, Colonel?''

''We've known worse times,'' Sam muttered. **And will again,** he thought.

Old Black Beaver's trail north through the Indian Nations into Kansas was an irregular sort of affair. Cattle herds had only traveled the route regularly the past two summers, but the bleached bones of horses and steers marked the path better than notched trees or signposts might have done. The bones and the occasional plank crosses of fallen cowboys served to remind the living of the perils surrounding them and those waiting up ahead. The veterans sang as they rode, and at night they swapped tales of other drives and remembered companions.

''Yonder's where ole Jesse Fletcher fell,'' one would say, pointing to a nearby ravine.

''Ole Shadow broke a leg on that prairie-dog hill,'' another soon added. ''Best cow pony I ever rode.''

The younger hands remained silent. They shared a sort of awestruck reverence. Their faces reflected hard times and sorrow for fallen friends, but they'd learned not to let their hearts linger too long on death or pain. They'd known too much of both already.

Those boys were quick learners, though, Sam discovered.

The reduced crew forced even the youngest to take a turn at night guard, and everyone was expected to run strays back to the main body. At first the veterans grumbled at the ignorance of the "hairless wonders."

"That Watt kid can't even stay in his saddle!" Morg Delaney complained. "Lord, he falls off his horse every mile or so. What's worse, he don't know a rope from an oak tree!"

A week later it was Morgan himself trimmed Elijah Watt's saddle so it would fit him better, and Bobby McDowell had the boy out tossing a lasso every other night after supper.

"They're comin' 'long," Chance Cooper observed after the outfit made a clean crossing of the South Canadian. "But now we're comin' into Kiowa and Comanche territory. Bet we'll wish we had a few chin whiskers among us soon."

In the end, the Trident crew managed to keep pace with two large herds from South Texas between the South Canadian and the Cimarron rivers. Hostile bands did appear twice, but they kept a respectable distance from the well-armed Texans.

North of the Cimarron, the South Texas outfits pulled ahead. Sam did his best to drive the men hard, but there were only so many hours in a day, and a few of them were needed to sleep and eat. The weather turned sour, too. A thunderstorm painted the sky bright with amber flashes of lightning, and the nervous steers threatened to stampede again. Twice the animals along the flanks surged into motion, but both times the hands managed to blunt the movement and prevent the kind of mad scramble that had so drastically reduced the original herd.

Beyond the Cimarron new menaces appeared. First a band of Kansas farmers appeared and denied passage to the Trident herd.

"Texas cows bring Texas ticks," a somber-faced gentleman explained. "Your animals are used to 'em, but they'll kill our stock off faster'n a flapjack fries on a hot griddle."

"Go 'round our land or be buried in it," a sour-faced old man challenged.

"Man as old as you ought not to be still livin'," Delaney replied. "Maybe it's you should eat some o' that precious Kansas dirt."

"Come now," Sam called, waving Delaney away from the confrontation. "Needn't come to blows over this business. It's just three days longer turning west and coming in that way."

"Three days'll put us even farther back o' the others, Colonel Delamer," Bobby McDowell pointed out. "Be August. Late for our bonus."

"We can blow our way right through these hayseeds," Delaney added. "Colonel, if you didn't want the use o' my Colts, why bring me 'long? There's other cowboys better'n I'll ever be."

"You know why you're here." Sam spoke slowly, cautiously. "And there could be need of your services, Morg. But not shooting Kansas farmers. For one thing there's hundreds of them. For another, they control the courts in this state. Night riders can empty many a saddle, but they only survive if they can outrun a posse. A trail crew can't."

Sam reluctantly honored the farmers' quarantine line and turned west. Other outfits avoided the quarantine by setting a roundabout course for Wichita in the first place. Those extra miles were a plague of frustration for the Trident crew. Then, when only two days short of the Arkansas and just a hair west of Wichita, riders appeared.

"Look there, Colonel," A. C. Dimmett called, pointing to three slender figures approaching from the north.

"Could be buyers," Sam said, studying the men for some hint of their purpose.

"Not them three," Morgan Delaney announced as he galloped over. "One in the middle's called Frenchy King. Runs a lot o' cattle to market, but he's yet to trail a herd."

"Rustlers?" Sam asked.

"Among the best, Colonel. He's handy with that pistol o' his, too, and he's sure to have more'n two men for company."

Sam nodded his agreement and studied the surrounding terrain. To the east and west low ravines offered perfect cover, and up ahead some low, cottonwood-studded hills offered high ground from which to launch a charge.

"Which way would you do it, Morg?" Sam asked, pointing out the possibilities.

"I'd use the ravines, then charge in on the outriders and pick them off. And I'd do it," Delaney explained, "when I had the others' attention by ridin' in from the front."

"That figures," Sam agreed. "You and Chance take one of the flanks each then. I'll—"

"Colonel, that McDowell fellow's steady. I passed him word an hour back to keep on the lookout. He's got the left point already. Chance can watch the right. The real trouble's sure to come from Frenchy, and it's there you'll need me."

"Don't figure I'm up to it, eh?" Sam asked, grinning.

"Not your kind o' fight, Colonel," Delaney answered with a like grin. "I'll bring 'em on in close, then you take 'em with that shotgun you keep under the seat. I'll drop Frenchy myself. We got a score needs settlin' from his time down on the Colorado. Time I earned my pay, ain't it?"

"I'd say so," Sam replied grimly. "Bring them along, Morg."

Delaney answered with a mock salute, then set off to pass the word to Chance Cooper and then meet the approaching outlaws.

It seemed like a simple plan, and Sam expected it to work as quickly as Morgan Delaney had said. But Frenchy King wasn't one to step quietly to death's door. The instant the rustler saw Morg Delaney, he raised a war whoop, and the flanks exploded with an outpouring of gunfire. Before Sam knew it, two of the outriders were down, and the cattle rumbled ahead out of control.

"Blast you, King!" Delaney shouted as he chased King and his two companions along the herd's right flank.

It was Chance Cooper thought to drive the stampeding steers into the nearest ravine. There, contained by the steep walls, the cattle found their progress slowed. Moreover, those rustlers lying in ambush there were driven from hiding or else savagely trampled.

On the left side, where the rustlers struck first, Bobby McDowell and two other hands sought to fend off a pair of mounted raiders. The two groups exchanged rifle shots, but dust obscured targets, and though there was considerable firing, nothing came of it.

Two other riders raced for the cook wagon. Sam waited patiently while Dimmett kept the wagon rolling. Then, as the outlaws pulled alongside, Sam swung his shotgun to bear and blew the eager rustlers to pieces. Faces and chests seemed to melt away, and what was left of the outlaws fell to the dusty Kansas plain.

"Got 'em, Colonel!" Dimmett cried. "There's two won't bother us again."

"Two," Sam grumbled as the danger of the moment dawned. "Too many of them left."

"Not so many," Dimmett observed as first one and then the other of King's accompanying horsemen fell. Delaney then steadied his hand and blasted Frenchy King from the saddle as well.

If the outfit had been a little more experienced or if Sam had ridden out to take charge, the rustlers might not have profited from their crime. But things being as they were, the remaining cowboys couldn't stem the stampede. Cattle broke out of the ravine and swept north and west while others scattered eastward. The surviving outlaws simply mounted their horses and drove along groups of steers as they fled.

The Trident outfit was powerless to prevent it. Sam, left far behind in the cook wagon by the rushing cattle, could do little but help Dimmett tend the wounded. The first two hit,

Roger Simpson and a Jack County boy known only as Whisper, lay in the midst of the scarred prairie, their bones trampled by the stampeding beeves.

"Hope the bullets took 'em," Chance Cooper spoke for all. "Be a hard way to die, bein' run down by a thousand head o' longhorns."

Aside from odd flesh wounds and general fatigue, the only other wounded were Elsworth Tidings, who took a bullet through one arm, and young Elijah Watt, who though he still hadn't grown a chin whisker, had dropped a pair of raiders before two bullets felled him.

"Boy's got heart," Dimmett announced as he did his best to stitch together the youngster's lacerated left ear. "Bit better aim on the part o' that rustler, and he'd be shy a brain, though."

"Never knew much o' anybody to think I was born with one," Watt said, wincing as the needle reunited two pieces of lobe. "Figure it'll mar my manly looks, Colonel?"

Sam shook his head. The ear was sure to mend fast enough. More serious was a bloody hole in the youngster's side.

"You'll be a while mending, Lige," Bobby McDowell said, squeezing young Watt's hand. "Anybody we can write to say you'll be along a bit late."

"Nobody," the boy mumbled. "Was Whisper and Benny Harper. But they're dead."

"When you're finished, Dimmett, take the wounded along to Wichita. We'll collect the herd and follow."

"Sure, Colonel," the cook agreed. Chance Cooper then grabbed a spade and set off to dig a pair of graves on the far hillside.

"Ain't much of us left to round up the cows," Delaney pointed out. "We could grab some boys in Wichita to help."

"There aren't many cows left to round up," Sam explained. "And no money to pay other hands."

Sam Delamer finally drove six hundred head to the stockyards in Wichita. He ached from ten straight hours atop a horse, and the others showed signs of the strain as well. The meager herd was a sore disappointment, but worst news lay ahead.

"Why, Sam, I didn't know you were trailing steers this year!" Lambert Perkins of Kansas City exclaimed when Sam approached the steps of the Kansas Hotel.

"Didn't you get my wire?" Sam asked. "I agreed to the price you quoted in April."

"I got a wire, Sam, but it said nothing of the sort," Perkins explained as he met the cattleman on the hotel porch. "It said you would have no stock to sell this summer. I don't understand how—"

"I understand," Sam said, clawing the splintery oak porch rail. "Wire come from Jacksboro, did it?"

"That's right. On the military telegraph, in point of fact."

"Well, it appears someone's played a fine trick on us, Lambert. At any rate, I still have six hundred head to sell you. They've been run some, but they're prime quality."

"Six hundred, Sam? You had some trouble, I take it."

"All manner of hardship topped off by Frenchy King's boys just shy of Arkansas. His men drove off a couple of hundred steers, I'd say, but we killed a fair number of the scoundrels, King among them."

"Well, there's some comfort in knowing the wicked have been dealt with. Sam, I can't buy your cattle. I've filled my needs. In fact, I leave tomorrow on the eastbound train."

"Maybe you can recommend me to one of your colleagues."

"Isn't anybody here," Perkins explained. "Oh, one or two fellows are over in Newton, I understand, and there are buyers in Abilene."

"I suppose we could send some wires."

"Of course we can, Sam. I'll do it personally. Why don't you get your men attended to? You all appear worse for the wear."

"We are," Sam grumbled. "Much worse."

Lambert Perkins sent wires to every stockyard along the Atchison, Topeka & Santa Fe Railroad, hoping to locate a buyer. No one responded.

"Sorry, Sam," Perkins said as he sat across from Sam at the dinner table that night. "I feel responsible for this situation. You've always delivered in the past, and we're certain to want your cattle in future years."

"More than likely there won't be any future," Sam said, turning his wineglass with his nervous fingers. "We're saddled with the federal occupation, you know. I'm certain that it was the same people who are taxing us to distraction that sent you that accursed telegram. These cattle are our cash crop, you know. I can barely pay my crew off as is, and the cattle will surely be seized to pay their feed and pen bills."

"No, they won't," Perkins answered. "I've bought stock most of my life, Sam, and I've never ventured into speculation before, but if you'll share the risk, I'll buy your beeves for twenty dollars a head and split the profit I receive when I sell them in Kansas City. Now, how does that sound?"

"Twenty dollars?" Sam asked. "That's low, Lambert."

"I know," the buyer confessed. "But twelve hundred dollars is all I have. If I get thirty-five or forty in Missouri, you'll have another five hundred or so coming as your share, though."

"That's true," Sam admitted.

"You won't find another offer, old friend. I've got the money in greenback dollars, too. No risk of a bank draft."

"Then I'd say we have an agreement," Sam said, clasping Perkins's hand. "I'll see papers are drawn up."

"I have a standard agreement in my bag down at the station. Why don't we sign things there. My train leaves in an hour, you know, and there are shipping details to attend to."

"Certainly," Sam said, rising with the buyer. "We should tend to it immediately."

"Yes, we should."

If Sam hadn't been worn down by his long ordeal and the

hours he'd suffered in the saddle, he might have insisted on a formal agreement stating the proposed terms of sale. Instead he signed the papers Lambert Perkins provided and saw the Kansas City buyer off on the late-evening eastbound.

"Collect the outfit," Sam told Morgan Delaney afterward. "I've sold the herd."

"Fine news, Colonel," Delaney replied. "I'll see the men are brought over."

As Sam handed out the promised pay he added an extra ten dollars as compensation for the hardships.

"I thought it might be more," Chance Cooper said. "Some o' the boys down at the Texas Saloon say they got fifty or a hundred."

"They were earlier," Sam explained. "Got a better price."

"Still, the low mark's close to fifty dollars a head, they say," Delaney argued. "And there's a buyer over in Newton promises fifty-five."

"What?" Sam asked as his fingers closed tightly on the stack of greenbacks.

"Didn't you know?" Delaney asked. "That fellow Perkins promised to pass the word on to you."

Sam's jaw began to shake, and it was only through extraordinary effort that he managed to hold his composure. Fifty-five? Like as not, that crook Perkins was selling the herd in Newton that very moment. And why not? Sam had signed the bill of sale. It was as clever a game as ever invented. If it didn't hurt so much, Sam would have managed a certain admiration.

"We sold somewhat less than that," Sam said. "But you boys are right. Fifty dollars will put a better shine on your boots."

"Three cheers for the colonel!" Bobby McDowell called, and the others howled their approval. Afterward, Sam drew Morgan Delaney aside.

"I've got a man I want you to visit, Morg," Sam explained. "Lambert Perkins. You'll find him in Newton, just up the way. Before you kill him, I want him to understand it was me sent you. And I want him to go slow, and quiet."

"Yes, sir," Delaney said, grinning. "I'll find an alley, make it seem an Indian did it. Even got a knife I took off an Osage over at the bathhouse."

"When you finish, have a look at the gentleman's bags. He might well have some cash about him."

"That's robbery, Colonel," Delaney argued. "I'm no thief."

"Man owes me money, Morg. It's not stealing to recover what's owed you."

"No, guess not," Delaney agreed. "I'll have a look."

Sam nodded soberly two days later when the Wichita newspaper carried the tale of Lambert Perkins's dastardly murder near the Newton stockyards. He was less delighted to learn a large sum of money had been deposited earlier by the same Perkins, and it was thought the savage manner of the cattle buyer's death hinted the murderer might have been in search of those funds.

"Had a good look," Delaney explained. "Was only a bit of silver and two twenty-dollar gold pieces. Sorry, Colonel."

"You accomplished your purpose," Sam said bitterly. There would be no laughing at Sam Delamer in the back-room gaming houses of Chicago and Kansas City.

But the roll of greenbacks Sam carried in his pocket would barely pay autumn taxes on the ranch. For the first time the notion that the Trident Ranch might slip from his hands hammered its way into Sam's thinking. To lose the ranch was unthinkable. When they got home, Morg would have more errands to tend. This, after all, was a war Sam Delamer wouldn't allow himself to lose.

# CHAPTER 9

Travis Cobb returned home the last week of July after passing a week or so in the entertainment establishments of Newton, Kansas. He rode atop a speckled stallion bought off a shrewd Cherokee trader, and he was decked out in a fine tailored suit complete with a silk cravat that half choked him in the Texas heat.

Beside him rode his brothers Lester, Jesse, and Bobby. The four Cobbs were rarely in such high spirits. The two hundred steers they had sold at trail's end had brought in ten thousand Yankee dollars, even after a week's celebrating in Newton. With money, a man could hold his head tall and build a future.

"Can't wait to see Pa's face," Jesse said as he pulled up alongside Travis. "It's more money'n I thought there was in all creation. We can build the house better'n ever, buy us some good horses . . ."

"Shoot, maybe we ought to buy out Sam Delamer," Les suggested. "Figure they ever found all their cows?"

"I hope so," Travis replied. "A man like Sam's dangerous when he's on top o' things. You get him down, he's liable to do anything. Anything at all."

"You still feared o' him?" Bobby asked. "Why, he ain't so much. Shot me, but I healed sure enough."

"Might not next time," Travis warned. "Let's have no more Delamer talk. This is a day to celebrate. We'll be home shortly, and I won't spoil such a glad time with sour words."

"Sure, Trav." Les spoke for the three younger brothers. "Let's talk about how we're goin' to spend all this money."

They did just that as the horses covered the last three miles to the ranch. Along the way they passed abandoned farms and unplanted fields. Then, as they cautiously completed the long journey by trotting along the market road across the Trident Ranch, they noticed the neglected fences, the pasture full of stray, unattended stock, a world grown seemingly empty.

"Where've all the people gone?" Jesse asked, scratching his head.

"It's like a plague's come and carried everybody off in the night," Les added. "Can things be so bad people've just given up and left?"

"Pray it's been better for Pa," Travis said, frowning. " 'Cause this ain't bad times. This puts me in mind o' the Shenandoah after ole Sheridan finished with her. That country was so sweet you could taste it. Afterward was just ashes and smoke."

When they reached the old wooden gate that had survived Comanche raids and civil war, Travis quickened the pace. Soon they rode past the barn to the one-room cabin that was serving as a temporary home. Before Travis could roll off his horse, Edna was racing to his side. Old Art waved and shouted his greetings. Little Davy, who'd turned ten in his brothers' absence, raced over from behind the chicken coop, shouting like a rooster at dawn.

"Lord, it's good to see you boys come home safe," Art said as he warmly greeted each of his sons in turn. "There's been letters arrived with sad new o' boys dead and buried."

"Oh?" Travis asked. "Not from our outfit, were they? Ted Slocum got back in one piece, didn't he?"

"Was by here three days back takin' his cousin into Fort Worth to buy some new clothes," Art explained. "The Finches got in yesterday. No, it seems like the youngsters hired on with Sam Delamer got hit hard, though. Stampede and then rustlers."

"Can't find any tears for a Delamer," Bobby said, scowling.

"Never a Delamer gets buried," Art answered. "Sam was short o' crew, so he took on 'bout anybody who could pull up his britches and sit a pony."

"His own fault," Travis declared. "He never treated folks right. If he lost steers on the way north, he had a bad habit o' makin' up the loss by means o' his neighbors. Last winter he sent good men packin' when the first norther hit. Men got memories, Pa."

"Truth is," Les argued, "Sam should've hired a good man to ramrod his herd. Instead he signed on that back-shootin' Morgan Delaney."

"If he hadn't chased Willie off, he wouldn't've had the need," Travis said bitterly.

"I knew some o' those boys rode with him," Bobby said, sadly gazing northward. "Swam the Brazos with Lige Watt and Benny Harper."

"Benny drowned at Red River," Art told the fourteen-year-old. "I've heard the Watt boy's still on the trail."

"Be hard on Lige, headin' north all alone," Bobby mumbled as he eyed his brothers. "Ain't easy, that trail."

"No, but it's got its rewards," Travis said, removing his money belt and passing it to his father. Art felt the weight and stared in disbelief.

"Ten thousand dollars, Pa!" Les exclaimed. "Enough to build a new house and buy furniture. We can sink that new well, and we can—"

"Spend some, and save the rest," Art announced. "Man

never goes too far wrong that way. You figure Ted Slocum did as well, Trav?''

"As well?'' Travis asked. "Why, he sold better'n two thousand head. He's a rich man, Pa. Must own a bank or two.''

"He said he had a proposition for you. Be back through on the way home. I asked him to supper tomorrow night. He and his pretty cousin both.''

"Thought she was married, Pa,'' Travis pointed out. "Has a boy.''

"Believe she still does, son, but she lost the husband. Ted said she was eager to make your acquaintance.''

The others greeted this news with a hoot or two, and Travis grew a bit purple around the face.

"Well, it's about time somebody brought a filly by for you, Trav,'' Les said, laughing. "Not gettin' any younger, you know.''

Travis gave Les a halfhearted whack on his seat and then lifted Davy onto one shoulder.

"You went and growed tall, little brother,'' Travis declared. "Had a birthday, I'm thinkin'. Figure to've earned a present or two?''

"I'll take the money belt,'' Davy answered, and the others laughed wildly. Jesse then opened up Travis's saddlebags, and it was Christmas in July. Davy got the lion's share of the loot, but Edna and Art did fair. By sundown word had spread of the Cobbs' homecoming, and half the county celebrated with a barn dance and barbecue.

The next evening Ted Slocum appeared as promised. Slocum was decked out like the man of property the drive had made him, and a fine matched pair of grays pulled his new canopied carriage.

"Got somethin' against horses, Ted?'' Travis asked as he observed the carriage.

"Oh, it's for Irene and the boy,'' Slocum explained. He then introduced his widowed cousin and her six-year-old.

"Pa was kilt in Arkansas fightin' the Yankees," the child explained. "Ma an' me been livin' with Uncle Ted lately."

"First chance the either of 'em's had to look 'round the country," Slocum pointed out. "Irene's been in Fort Worth the last month, doin' a bit o' sewin' and such. Had Mike here in school."

"Doin' my figures," the boy said with a frown. "I'd rather ride horses."

"Time for the both," Travis announced. "Come along in, Ted. Edna's got supper waitin'."

"Can't have that," Irene said. "Leave it to men to jaw away and ruin a good meal."

It was a good meal, for there was plenty of beef left from the barbecue, and Edna had roasted some ears of corn and mashed a platterful of potatoes. Mint tea topped off the meal, together with blackberries and cream.

While Irene entertained Edna with tales of Fort Worth's finery, Jesse and Bobby tackled the dishes. Art walked off to smoke his pipe, and Ted Slocum led Travis toward the creek.

"I remember the day the major led us through here," Slocum said, gazing at the break in the tall cliffs that marked the passing of the Brazos. "Was hard, comin' all that way through the defeated South, seein' so much hunger and despair, all the near-naked orphans and the burned-out cabins. For a time it seemed it was turnin', gettin' better. Lately this country looks worse'n ever."

"We've money to rebuild now," Travis said.

"Sam'll have money, too, when he sells his beef. There's no room to grow here, Trav. Only an invitation to get Delamer-strangled."

"Pa says so, too."

"Why don't you take your profits and buy that acreage I was tellin' you about. It's full o' mustangs and longhorns just waitin' for a man to rope and make 'em his. I did as much myself, Trav, and I've come to be rich."

"I never been a good loser, Ted. This is my home!"

"Well, that's a thought, but have you ever looked at how this place is goin' to support you and four brothers besides?"

"Be a time before Bobby and Davy grow to size," Travis said, laughing.

"And when they do, the cavalry'll've chased the Comanches to perdition. Once the Indians're gone, this western country's bound to open up fast. You may not be able to buy a decent spread then, and you sure won't have the stock there waitin', free as the wind."

"Maybe you're right about the future, Ted. Maybe not. But I don't suppose it would hurt to look into buying the land. What do you suppose it would cost?"

"It's gone for as little as four bits an acre. A dollar's more likely. Most of it's deeded, but the county's taken it for taxes. Pay what's due and a bit besides, and you'd have a nice stretch o' land."

"I'll visit with Pa on it. Maybe he and the boys could go on up there."

"And you?"

"I got some fightin' yet to do," Travis explained.

Slocum returned to the hovel of a cabin then, and Travis made his way through the scrub oaks to the creek. He tossed flat stones in the shallow water awhile before he realized someone was watching.

"I used to do that myself," Irene said, skipping a stone three times before it hopped onto the far bank. "Sometimes I take Mike down to the river, and we have a try."

"None too safe, a woman and a boy out in that country alone," Travis observed. "Comanches don't mind takin' scalps, and they value the pretty blond ones most of all."

"I take that for a compliment," she said, grinning. "Of course, Ted always has somebody watching us. He's a worrier."

"Has a right," Travis told her. "Seen some worrisome things, we have."

"You two served together in the war. He talks of it often."

"Not me. I try to forget."

"Do you?"

"Altogether?" he asked. "No, I guess not."

"Neither do I. George wasn't but nineteen when he died. He never even saw Mike. I suppose Mike was sort of my parting gift, or maybe George's. It's a comfort knowing something survived."

"Sometimes. I'm not always sure when I pass through towns with orphans beggin' work or else livin' off what they can steal. Haven't left 'em much of a life, we soldiers."

"What about your life, Travis? Is it enough?"

"From time to time it is. Not what I expected, though. When I was younger, my sister Ellie and I used to make all sorts o' wishes, especially on the evenin' star. Might've come true, some o' them, if . . . well, that's another tale. This is a fine time, and I don't want to spoil it by raisin' bitter subjects."

"No, let's not do that," she agreed. "Travis, do you suppose you would mind taking my hand? It's been ages since I walked along the creek with a handsome young man."

"Handsome?" he asked, laughing. "Never been called that, and as to young, I'm not even that anymore. But I'd surely give you a walk, ma'am. A Southern gentleman is always on call when needed."

They strolled along the bank together once, twice, three times. Travis felt himself grow oddly warm at her touch. It was eerie, that glow growing inside him. Something half-forgotten seemed to awake from long slumber. He finally stopped, then turned her face and tenderly kissed her lips.

"It's been a long time for me, too," she whispered as she returned the kiss. "I'd hate to think it will be so long before the next time."

"It won't be," Travis promised as he clasped her hands. "That is, if you wouldn't mind my payin' you a visit."

"There's a camp meeting this Sunday down at the forks of the Brazos," she explained. "A picnic afterward. I'll expect you."

"Be there if I can," he responded.

# CHAPTER 10

Ψ

Sam Delamer's homecoming was in stark contrast to the that of his neighbors. It had taken ten days to make the roundabout journey through Kansas and Missouri by train and thence through Arkansas and Texas via stagecoach. Another man would have ridden south through the Nations. Indeed, others had. Sam turned green at the mere notion of so many miles bobbing atop a horse.

Morgan Delaney, Chance Cooper, and the surviving trail hands celebrated a bit in Wichita and thus only beat their employer home by a day or two. Little Elijah Watt, having developed pneumonia in a damaged lung, had coughed out his life in the surgery of a Wichita doctor. That boy, like his young companions, lay in a shallow Kansas grave.

As Sam stepped out of the dusty coach at the Brazos crossing a mile west of the ranch, he still couldn't shake the haunting stare of that boy from his mind. The eyes might have been little Charlie's, for the unspoken truths were akin. Sam Delamer had failed to fend off the hand of death once again. And now, with scarcely enough cash money to keep the ranch alive through Christmas, he wondered whether his own children might not greet their father with similar gazes.

"Wasn't anybody expectin' you in today, Colonel Delamer," Toliver Cotes, who managed the way station, observed as he supervised the unloading of Sam's baggage. "Ain't anybody from the ranch been by."

"They didn't know," Sam growled. "I'll borrow a horse if it's convenient and send it back afterward."

" 'Course, Colonel," Cotes agreed. "Got a fine chestnut geldin' in the corral jest as gentle's a lamb child. Get you along home just fine."

"Thank you," Sam said, ignoring the grin on the stationman's face. It was well known Sam was no horseman, and he had no intention of proving anything by selecting a rogue stallion or a rock-rumped mule for the sake of pride.

"Got some letters here for you, too, Colonel," Cotes's boy Jefferson called as Sam headed for the corral. "Look important, some of 'em. From Austin and such."

"Thank you, son," Sam said, taking the letters and passing a shiny silver dollar into the thirteen-year-old's hands. "Save somebody a trip. As for the bags, I'll send a wagon back for them. When they return the chestnut."

"I'll see they're not bothered," Jefferson pledged. "As if there was anybody hereabouts to mess with anything."

Sam laughed at the youngster's scowl. If not for Fulton, that station would even now rest on Delamer land, and the stage would halt its progress at the big house. Now? Who knew?

Sam covered the final mile of his long journey slowly. In his mind he rehearsed the words he would exchange with Helen, how he would explain the bitter failure and the calamities that had marred the Trident crew's northern journey. He thought of the disappointed faces of the little ones. There were no fine presents this year, no promises of buying trips to Fort Worth. Robert would expect a saddle pony. Well, it was well that boy didn't have everything handed to him. It was the struggle built character, after all.

As he rode along the river Sam gazed at the sorry state of

the ranch. The cattle were horribly scattered, and fences were down in a dozen places. Last spring no one could have ridden long on Trident range without being challenged. Now Sam rode to within a few hundred yards of the house itself before Matt Cooper appeared.

"Why, it's the colonel!" the young man called. "Chance, look who's gotten back!"

The elder Cooper emerged from a live-oak thicket, and Sam kicked his horse into a slow trot.

"Got back all right, I see," Sam observed. "Morg come with you?"

"He and a few others," Chance explained. "Colonel, word's got out we had trouble. Half the hands pulled out, and there's scarce enough left to finish brandin'."

"What?" Sam cried. "Finish branding? That should have been done long ago."

"Ain't been," Matt said, joining his cousin and their employer. "Had some Indian trouble to begin with. Got a man arrow-shot. Then payday come, and there was no money."

"I left funds," Sam said, gazing angrily toward the house. "You boys pass the word. I'll see the men paid before supper."

"Yes, sir," Matt answered with a whoop. "Knew you'd stand by the men, Colonel. I'll tell the rest."

As Matt turned away to spread the news Sam scowled. "Know what's passed, Chance?" he asked.

"No, Colonel. I'd suspicion somebody's spent a bit freely on horses, though. There's some new ones in the barn. Fine animals, mind you, but they couldn't've come cheap."

"Yes," Sam said, remembering the affection Clay Stanpole had for horseflesh. It was fine to indulge in whims when you had money. When times were lean, it was best to pull the money strings tight. "Chance, when your cousin gets back, take this gelding back to Cotes. Fetch my baggage along home, and leave young Jefferson this silver dollar. He's a good boy, that one. Has good ears, too."

"I understand, Colonel," Cooper replied as he accepted the coin. "Might have a visit with him afterward."

"Fine notion, Chance. Ask about Judge Fulton in particular."

"Consider it done, sir."

Chance then turned his horse toward the barn. Sam, on the other hand, trotted up to the house and turned the gelding over to a pair of idle stableboys.

"Welcome back, Colonel," Ollie Griffin declared. "Jerome, you go warn Matthew, hear!"

The second boy ran off toward the house. Moments later little Sam raced Catherine to their father's side. Sam lifted each in an arm and embraced them warmly. Robert followed, gazing around expectantly. When he discovered his father was alone, he extended a hand.

"Welcome home, sir," the nine-year-old said. "We missed you."

"Indeed we did," Helen added as she made her way down the broad steps and joined the reunion. "We had begun to worry, dear. Such tales you hear!"

"It was a hard drive," Sam said as he shook himself loose from the youngsters and held his wife closer. "Where's Clayton?"

"In your office," she answered. "With company."

"Oh?" he asked.

"James is home," she said, trembling slightly.

"I wouldn't have expected him to visit in August," Sam said, sharing her concern.

"I summoned him," she explained. "I didn't know what else to do. There was money due, and—"

"Quite the right thing, I'd judge, Helen. We'll talk more of it later. For now, I'd best have a word with my brother."

"Don't you want to wash first?" Robert asked. "Matthew's hurrying a bath."

"It can wait a few minutes," Sam said, pausing long enough to rest a hand on his eldest son's shoulder. "You look to have kept your mama, sister, and brothers well, Robert. I'm proud of you."

"Yes, sir," the boy said, nodding shyly.

Sam then excused himself and marched to the office. He threw the door open and stepped inside. Clayton Stanpole sat behind the desk, his polished boots propped on a table. James sat across the way, together with State Senator Olin Preston.

"Excuse my abrupt entrance, gentlemen," Sam said, making a half bow toward the senator as he fought to swallow his anger. "I've just returned from—"

"Yes, Sam, how are you?" the senator said, extending his right hand. "I've just been sharing news of your misfortunes with young Stanpole here."

"Welcome home, Sam," James added, nodding respectfully toward his older brother. Stanpole squirmed a bit as he quickly set his feet on the floor.

"So, you seem to have told everyone else the state of the ranch, Clayton," Sam announced. "Why not bring me up to date?"

"Well, Sam, we've had some troubles," Clayton began. He elaborated how Judge Fulton had imposed a new tax that had snatched a thousand dollars, and certain projects hadn't turned the expected profits.

"I understand there are some new horses," Sam noted.

"I got them for a fine price down in Waco," Stanpole answered. "Ought to improve the line considerably."

"At what expense?" Sam asked.

"Three thousand dollars," James answered. "He's gone and paid double the going rate for animals we've no hope of selling west of Kentucky. Sam, I had to borrow against my books in order to raise payroll. I hope you sold the cattle at a profit."

"Not a great one," Sam said, eyeing his brother-in-law coldly. "You owe me already, Clay. Now twofold. I see debts are repaid me, don't I, Senator?"

"He's a man to keep his promises, son," Preston acknowledged.

"Now, let's set aside that for the moment. It's ideal you've come, Olin. You too, James. Because just now we've got a problem needs solving. It goes by the name of Judge DeWitt Fulton."

"That's a sizable fish to tackle," Preston declared. "He's got tremendous resources, Sam. Money, connections."

"What connections?" Sam asked.

"Oh, for one thing, he has the ear of Senator Sherman in Washington. That's Atlanta Billy Sherman's brother, you understand. For another, he got that fool Schuyler Colfax into politics. Colfax just so happens to be vice-president at present. Sherman puts the army in his pocket. Colfax puts the government there alongside. And he's salted away a share of every tax dollar paid in his section of Texas."

"Even so, he's bound to have a weak link," Sam argued. "What have you found, James?"

"A fair trail of purchases," James answered. "I've found money transferred between banks, but it's not much use as a weapon. Records catch fire, you know, and who's going to try a federal judge for stealing from Rebels?"

"Doesn't Delamer money buy help anymore?" Sam asked.

"What money, Sam?" James asked. "We're near broke."

"Then we'll have to use other tactics," Sam declared.

"Maybe Senator Preston would like a look at those new horses," James said, nodding soberly. "Clay, you'll take him around, won't you?"

"I think I should sit in on this discussion," Stanpole objected. "After all, I'm manager of the ranch, aren't I?"

"Mismanager would be more like it," James muttered.

"Come along, young man," Senator Preston urged. "Show me those horses."

"Sam?" Stanpole appealed.

"Go on, Clay," Sam insisted. "Take your time, too. I'll be handling the ranch accounts personally from now on."

"Sure," Stanpole said, sighing as he led the senator toward the door. Once they had departed, James drew from his pocket a batch of papers.

"It won't be easy, Sam, but I think there might just be a way," the younger Delamer explained. "I've got a friend, Martin Tyler, in Austin. We studied together two years. His cousin Pat happens to be Judge Fulton's clerk."

"Sure, I've met the boy."

"Pat's no fool. He knows plenty of law, and he's fair with figures. I'd wager he can get enough evidence. After all, a clerk knows everything that comes in and out of a court."

"Then what?"

"I've made myself an acquaintance in Jacksboro. The new federal marshal, Coke Lindsay."

"Go on."

"He hasn't got much affection for Fulton. That judge has him off running people off their land, collecting taxes, and Fulton never shares a cent of the take. Moreover, Lindsay's been shot twice from ambush!"

"And?"

"He told me he'd rather enjoy making Fulton a prisoner in his own jailhouse. For a price, that is."

"Anything for a price, eh?" Sam asked, grinning. "You can count on a man who's apt to benefit from a common project."

"I took the liberty of inviting Baldy Nichols up from Austin, too."

"The cattlemen's detective?" Sam asked.

"You heard of him then. He worked for the Pinkertons in Kansas till he got too handy with his shotgun. Now he's grown clever in his dealings. We've had a talk or two, and he's got an idea."

"I'm glad someone does."

"You didn't send me to study the law without a notion I'd

prove of value, did you?" James asked, the smile falling from his face. "No, Sam, it wasn't for my health, was it? Well, I've learned well enough to have my license."

"Congratulations, little brother," Sam said, offering his hand.

"You keep your hand, Sam. I'm not saving the ranch for you. It's part mine, too, you know. Once this is over, I expect to profit considerably. Don't sulk now, Sam. There will be plenty for everyone, even after we pay off our friends. I've already made arrangements to move my things to Jacksboro. I took a lease on a house just off Main Street on the old Belknap military road. From there I can watch the court-house and the fort."

"I'm impressed. So, little . . . So, James, what's my role to be?"

"What it's always been. Keep after the neighbors, lull the judge into the illusion he's won."

"Feint to the right and slash with the left, eh?" Sam asked.

"Works every time," James said, rising. "So long as we keep our tactics secret. Especially from that fool of a brother-in-law. Sam, how could you leave him in charge of the ranch? He's got no head for reason, and he talks too much when he drinks."

"Oh, he serves a purpose now and then," Sam said, rubbing his chin. "He can be manipulated. My mistake was leaving him cash to play with. I won't make that mistake twice."

"Do we have any money left?"

"Enough, I think," Sam said. "If we don't waste too much time."

"I won't. I plan to get started today."

"James, you watch yourself in these dealings. A man who will betray one man will certainly do so again."

"Don't you worry yourself about that," James assured him. "I'm not Willie. I don't altogether trust anybody."

Sam Delamer had little chance to settle in at the ranch. Once he paid the ranch hands and bid farewell to James and the senator, other visitors appeared. First came a bluecoat cavalry column. Afterward DeWitt Fulton arrived.

"Bring word of another tax levy, Judge?" Sam asked as he greeted the Ohioan.

"No new levy," the judge answered with a grin.

"Come to steal horses or cattle then?"

"No, I've acquired those elsewhere. I just thought you'd like your autumn tax bill. It's a heavy one, and I thought you deserved a personal delivery this time around."

"I guess I should feel honored," Sam said, taking the papers from the judge. The total was far in excess of the funds on hand. Both men appeared to know that.

"Not short are you, Sam?" Fulton asked with a savage grin. "I would consider it such a shame to file against such a fine place as this."

"You'll have your money!" Sam barked.

"Ah, I'm certain of it. Convinced of it, Sam. Perhaps if not in cash, we could come to other terms. Shall we have a talk?"

"Come along to the office," Sam said reluctantly. "We won't likely be disturbed there."

"And could we share some refreshment? I'm afraid the trip out from Jacksboro always leaves me parched."

"Tea?" Sam asked.

"I believe you know me better," Fulton said, tapping an empty whiskey flask.

"I'll let Matthew know," Sam said, waving the judge toward the house.

A few minutes later they stood alongside Sam's map, sipping whiskey as the judge examined the Trident's boundaries.

"You've done some elaborate preparation, haven't you, old friend?" Fulton asked. "Pays a man to plan. Of course, some plans have to be postponed, don't they?"

"Yes, postponed," Sam agreed.

"You've quite a heritage here," Fulton continued, touching the cold steel on the ancient French sword. "I recall another visit I made here. Your brother, that Rebel major, had just come home. I had young Winthrop with me. You recall. He commanded the cavalry escort. Winthrop pulled a pistol and shot your brother through the toe, I believe, a sin for which your brother promptly returned fire, neatly putting a ball through Winthrop's head. Whatever became of that young devil?"

"Winthrop died," Sam said, shifting his weight uneasily.

"Oh, I know that. I meant your brother."

"He went north with me to Kansas," Sam explained. "To help with the cattle drive. Afterward, he drifted into the Dakotas. I tried to find out where he was afterward. Report I got was he was Sioux-scalped in the Big Horn country."

"Oh, I wouldn't set much faith in reports of that sort. News from that area is quite unreliable. I guess you'll never really know what became of him . . . unless he rides in for a visit. I suppose he'd be welcome, especially if he struck gold in that mountain country."

Sam cringed as the judge continued to examine the office.

"Now your other brother," Fulton continued, "James. He was the levelheaded one. He's bound for Jacksboro, you know. In point of fact, he's leased a house I own. I received a note from him today. It seems he and Martin Tyler are friends. Young Pat's my clerk, as you surely know. It will be nice, chatting with James, talking over old times. He knows a great deal . . . about things."

"Things?" Sam asked nervously.

"The history of the county, for example. The river and the people hereabouts. Fascinating subject."

"I thought you'd be too busy for such distractions," Sam declared. "After all, there are tax bills to make out."

"Most of that's done," Fulton insisted. "Besides, there's always time for important matters, Sam. Always. And no matter is more important than the future disposition of this fine ranch.''

Sam stood as still as possible. Inside he was fuming, and his face grew alternately pale and crimson as Judge Fulton spoke of plans for a new, larger ranch.

''I always liked you, Sam,'' Fulton said as he turned toward the door. ''I respect a man who puts success ahead of principle. We've done some business, the two of us. But there's only room for one king on this river. And we both know who that will be.''

''Do we?'' Sam asked.

''We will soon,'' Fulton boasted. ''Very soon.''

# CHAPTER 11

Ψ

Autumn found Palo Pinto County unchanged. Still the people suffered under their heavy burdens, but the end of the summer heat seemed to blow a fresh breeze across the land. And as farmers harvested corn and vegetables, they rekindled hopes of better times ahead.

Travis Cobb supervised the plucking of the corn from stalks high as his forehead, and afterward the family watched with rare satisfaction as the cribs filled to bursting.

"Be a good year, I'm thinkin'," old Art declared. "Got cash to pay the taxes and plenty o' corn to keep the hogs and kids content. Yup, sure to be a good year."

Travis thought so as well, though perhaps not for the same reason. More and more his attentions were turned west, to Ted Slocum's place. When time permitted it, he and Irene Milligan rode horses along the Brazos. Sometimes they would pass an afternoon skipping rocks. Twice each month they'd attend Reverend Ames's camp meetings and picnic afterward with little Mike down on the riverbank.

"I've been a lifetime alone," Travis confessed toward the first week of October. "Most o' that time I been fightin' one war or another. Not much softness in between. I can't offer anybody much save for my pure devotion and the best life these two gnarled hands can make.''

"Go on," Irene encouraged.

"You're a better woman than I've rights to've crossed paths with, Irene," Travis told her. "Better'n I thought was left in this troubled world. I got my faults, and I'm known to be ill-tempered, but if you'd take me for your husband, I'd give you my best."

"I know you would, Trav," she replied. "I feel for you, too. But there are things to consider."

"Things?" he asked.

"Mike," she explained. "He's . . ."

"Best marry him, Mama," the youngster cried from a hiding place back of a forked live oak. "Ain't too many 'round for you to choose. And 'sides, he can throw a rock 'cross a river just fine."

"You heard him," Travis said, grinning as the wisp of blond hair appeared and disappeared behind the tree. "Can't argue with the logic o' that."

"Guess I can't," she said, clasping his hands. "So I suppose I'd best say yes."

They were wed two weeks later, on a bright but chilly first Sunday morning in November. Reverend Ames read the vows as a prelude to the meeting he held near Palo Pinto, and the county turned out in full force and fine feather. Ted Slocum stood at Travis's elbow, to cut off retreat, some said. Meanwhile little Mike and his new uncles waited anxiously to shower the newlyweds with hard kernels of rice.

The Delamers, it was said, had taken a trip to Austin, but Chance and Matt Cooper brought a silver teapot and cups as a gift from the ranch.

"Colonel asked you to take it as an olive branch," Chance explained. "Sign 'o peace."

"Thank him," Travis said, accepting the handsome gift with a solemn nod. The teapot was considerably more valuable than Sam Delamer's pledge.

Ellen and Jack Trent had come down from Wise County for the day. It was their first visit since Ellen had given birth in late spring, and she proudly showed off the plump, wide-eyed child.

"I knew it would be a boy," she told her father. "A tall one like his grandfather."

"Hope he's got more o' his pa's sense than my size," Art suggested. "Be better off."

"Maybe we'll be lucky, and he'll wind up with both," she said, smiling.

When Travis and Ellen visited after the reverend's sermon, the subject turned to old times. They recollected other, better days. Then they spoke of Sam Delamer.

"Haven't heard much from him o' late," Travis admitted. "He's lyin' low, I guess."

"Ole Sam's got troubles of his own, as I hear it," Ellen said, swallowing hard. "He's at odds with that carpetbagger judge and the soldiers both. An agent for the ranch conducted a sale in Decatur, and I wager that teapot is about the last silver piece to leave Helen's hutch."

"He's that bad off?" Travis asked.

"So I'm led to understand. Before you start crying, I'd best add there's talk Judge Fulton plans to take over the Trident Ranch. If he does, it will be worse even than Sam. You know people say half our taxes never leave that judge's fingers. He's speculated on land, bought all sorts of railroad bonds, and now he appears ready to take a share of the stage line."

"Got some grand plans, that one," Travis remarked.

"He's got a determined enemy, too. I wouldn't paint him the winner just yet. You know Jamie's taken up the law in Jacksboro."

"I heard that," Travis said, nodding his head. "Every once in a while I see that boy."

"Except for the dark hair, he puts me in mind of Willie."

"You haven't altogether forgotten him, have you?" Travis

asked. "Not accidental you named the boy William. How's Jack feel about that?"

"He considers it fitting," she said, nodding sadly. "Named for the one who didn't come back."

"He did, once."

"But he didn't stay. Pity, that. We've gone on, haven't we, Trav? I admit, though, when I see Jamie, I'm reminded."

"They both got their mama's eyes," Travis pointed out. "Tall and lean, too."

"But they don't have Sam's hungry look."

"No, that family only bred one coyote."

"Don't be altogether certain," Ellen warned. "We've seen a lot of friends cheated out of their land up in Wise County. You run up against a sharp-eyed lawyer without the proper papers, and the next thing you know, you're walking barefooted with your family, hoping someone'll have enough pity to offer you food and a fire."

"I've got our titles in a safe place, Ellie," Travis promised. "And we've got money to hire our own lawyers."

"Be careful, big brother. Don't forget those hungry eyes."

"I never do," Travis told her.

In the weeks that followed, though, he was too busy building a cabin for Irene and young Mike down beside the creek to give Sam Delamer much thought. Three loads of lumber from Jerome Stone's sawmill had helped replace the main house, and a fourth was slowly hammered into shape at the creek.

"Seems like there was plenty o' room up here for everyone," Bobby complained as the Cobbs nailed plank after plank onto the framework. "Irene and Edna could share rooms, and Mike was welcome to come in with me and Davy."

"Fine chance we'd have for nephews that way!" Jesse complained. "You'll never make a horse breeder, Bob. Not if you bolt the mares up in the barn and send the stallions off to pasture."

Bobby grinned bashfully and tried to hide behind his hat. Travis only laughed and ordered the boys to work harder.

By Christmas both houses were finished, and the spirals of gray smoke rising from their chimneys attested to the warmth and contentment that found the Cobbs those last days of 1869. The hills were full of singing and fiddle playing, not to mention a celebration or two in honor of Art Cobb's two grandchildren.

"Ellie grew hers the hard way," the old man observed. "Trav here, he always was one to take the short way 'round."

"Well," Irene said as she drew Mike up onto her lap, "we didn't build a three-room house with a solitary child in mind."

"Glad to hear it!" Art said, tapping his foot on the wooden floorboards. "This county needs more Cobbs!"

"Hooray for that!" Les shouted.


A mile away, Christmas was a less joyous season. Sam Delamer gazed at walls suddenly grown bare and long shelves emptied by desperation sales. He'd sold the silver, several fine New Orleans tapestries, even his own gold watch. Even so, he'd barely met the tax bill. And now, with winter closing in, the children were growing thin from a diet of corn mush and beef.

Most of the ranch crew had departed. Two months' wages had gone unpaid, and promises weren't much to live on. Bobby McDowell and a handful of men with no place else to go remained, as did Clayton Stanpole. Amazingly the Coopers and Morgan Delaney stuck, too.

"Colonel's got plans," Delaney said often. "We'll come out just fine when all's said and done."

Sam withstood his own wants, and he endured the grins and gossip of the neighbors. He and Helen now avoided the bi-monthly camp meetings in Palo Pinto, and they spoke no more of the church and school they would build. Otherwise Sam held his head high and labored long and hard to find a solution to his troubles. It was only when the sullen faces of the children stared up at him Christmas morning that he felt himself waver.

"Just an orange, Papa?" Catherine asked. "Have I been bad?"

"Papa, my boots are near worn through and so small my feet hurt," Robert grumbled. "I didn't mean it about the horse, you know. It wasn't so important."

"You've got food to eat," Sam answered harshly. "There are children in this county going hungry, and close to freezing from the cold. None of you have ever known that kind of hardship. Do you good to miss a few presents."

James appeared an hour later with small bundles that salvaged a bit of the children's spirits. But the hugs and kisses awarded their uncle only gnawed at Sam.

"Maybe it's time to walk away from it all," Sam muttered when he and James examined the ranch accounts. "We can't go on this way much longer. I've sold nearly everything for which there was a buyer. There's nothing left."

"I've saved a few hundred dollars," James said. "It should see the ranch through the next few months. Till another cattle drive is organized."

"And just who will sign on with the Trident?" Sam asked. "People know we're not paying our crew now. The good cowboys heard what happened last year. And the youngsters recount that drive to scare their smaller brothers and sisters."

"None of that matters," James explained. "If we outlast Fulton, we'll be in high clover."

"And how will we do that, little brother?"

"By gritting it out," James declared. "You move Helen and the little ones to Jacksboro if you want. They'll see some real suffering there. A twelve-year-old boy froze to death in the livery stable just last week."

"You don't have children yet, Jamie," Sam said, using the pet version of his brother's name for the first time in two years. "I never intended they should know this sort of need."

"Don't you think I feel it, too?" James asked. "Don't you figure I have any pride? I'm a Delamer, too. Maybe I wasn't the oldest, and I never led a cavalry charge like Willie or fought Comanches like you, Sam, but I've lived the last third of my life an orphan, with nobody to show me the way or smooth the path! So before you go crying to me how heartless the world's gone and become, let me tell you it's never been all that soft for some of us."

"I haven't cried since Mama died," Sam said bitterly. "You'll never see me do it."

"You're about to quit. It's pretty much the same thing, Sam. Now you listen to me. I've planted seeds, and they'll take some time to blossom. Meanwhile, you have to stand fast. So long as Fulton's eyes are on you, he won't give me a second glimpse. I'm just a boy, after all, a young pup come up from Austin in his tailored clothes to read the law. I make claims against the soldiers for trampling Mrs. McCall's turnips or failing to pay their laundry tabs down at Sudsville. Sometimes I get a real opportunity, like defending Cyrus Applegate against a charge of stealing old Pop Bloom's prize rooster."

"How do you stand it?" Sam asked.

"Stand it?" James asked. "I thrive on it. Because one day soon that high and mighty Yank judge is going to fall hard, and when he looks over to see who's pulled the rug from under his boots, he'll find it's little Jamie Delamer. And I'll be grinning like a fox that just cleaned out a henhouse."

"I wish I shared your confidence, James."

"Might as well," the younger Delamer urged. "It doesn't cost anything."

That evening, after sharing a pair of plump geese shot by Bobby McDowell down at the river with the collected crew, Sam left the children to play with the hands. He and Helen sat beside the fireplace and spoke of other, better times.

"I always thought I could survive anything after the humiliation of the Yankees entering New Orleans," Helen said with a sigh. "Watching our Negroes set loose on the warehouses, having Yankee trash mock fine ladies and display their disgusting habits in front of young girls. And if a hand was raised against them, the body attached was sorely punished."

"I never thought I'd know as dark a time as the day I buried Charlie."

"That's because you didn't bury a father and three brothers in the war," she said. "This, though, is such a trial because there's no enemy to direct my hatred at. It's such a silent madness that's gripped our home. And I blame myself, especially for Christmas."

"You blame yourself?" Sam asked, gripping her shoulders. "Why, dear, that's nonsense. How could it be your fault?"

"I wrote Clayton and brought him here," she explained. "I entrusted him with the money, and I said nothing when he squandered it on foolishness. I know, too, you never would have made all those loans had I not implored you so. All that money, Sam! It's so needed now."

"Yes, indeed it is," Sam admitted. "But a year ago I would never have given it a second thought. This is my doing, Helen. My fault entirely."

They embraced in hopes of lending warmth and support, but not even the fire blazing beside them could shake off the growing chill or the encroaching gloom.

Later, as Sam rocked silently in the ancient oak chair built by his grandfather back in the twenties, Robert stepped quietly to his father's side.

"Papa, are you sick?" the boy asked. "Or just sad?"

"A little of both," Sam confessed as he helped Robert up onto one knee. The boy was growing, and he wasn't so light a load as in the past. There was something solid about his ribs, too.

"I've been thinking, Papa," Robert went on. "Maybe I could go out with Chance some, help mend some of the fences. I've been chopping stove wood, you know."

"No, I didn't," Sam said, gazing with surprise at the slender child that had always seemed too soft for frontier life.

**107**

"Matthew says there are lots of herbs and roots in the woods that are good to eat, too. We could maybe pick some so our gums won't bleed so."

"Your gums bleed?"

"Not so much," Robert said, staring at the floor. "Chance says he can help me make some moccasins, too, so we won't have to buy any boots after all."

"Bound to make you a regular frontiersman, is he?"

"Figure I'd look all right in a beaver hat?"

"I don't think there are many beavers hereabouts anymore, son. But in the early days, a lot of folks wore coonskin caps."

"Lots of coons down by the river."

"Maybe we'll get out my rifle and shoot you one."

"And you figure I can have a cowhide for the moccasins?"

"Promise you we'll fetch one first thing tomorrow."

"Papa, you won't stay sad long, will you?" Robert asked. "It makes Catherine and Sam unhappy. Me too. Even baby Stephen notices."

"No, I won't be sad long, son," Sam promised as he helped Robert onto the floor.

"And we'll shoot a coon soon as the clouds clear, huh?"

"That's a promise," Sam declared.


"I hear Christmas was a little short over at the Trident spread this year," Art Cobb told Travis that next morning. "Maybe we should've sent somethin'."

"Like what, Pa?" Travis asked. "A fire?"

"Food maybe. Or some blankets."

"Don't go stowin' away the shotguns just yet, Pa. You got to make mighty sure a coyote's dead 'fore you turn your back on him. Same goes for Delamers."

"Trav!"

"You heard me, Pa. It's a truth to take to heart. Wait and see. We haven't had our last tangle with those varmints yet."

# CHAPTER 12

A cold, terribly bitter January greeted Texas, and Sam Delamer couldn't help wondering if the weather wasn't a hint of the hard times that lay ahead for the Trident Ranch. It was unimaginable that the day could come when his children would be wearing cowhide moccasins and coonskin caps. It was a regression to primitive life, a hideous move backward for Brazos society.

The solitary cause for optimism during those dismal days was a buoyant James Delamer. The young man visited the ranch weekly, and even on those occasions when he appeared half-frozen, with frost turning his hair white, James always shook off the misery with a grin and offered a hopeful smile as he meted out hard candy for the children.

"It's time you make the trip next week," James told Sam as they met in the middle of the month. "I may have news. Either way there are things to consider. And plans to form."

"I'll come," Sam promised.

So he did, arriving in Jacksboro on an overcast Tuesday. He left Bobby McDowell to tend to the covered carriage and walked on to James's simple house down the street. He arrived there to find his brother gone.

*At courthouse*, a note in the window read.

Sam frowned. He didn't relish the notion of another meeting with DeWitt Fulton, especially one involving James. Yet standing alone on the porch, waiting who knew how long, didn't have much appeal, either. Finally Sam decided to walk on down the street to the courthouse.

The frame structure erected on the town square was far from the imposing buildings put up elsewhere. There wasn't much need, however. Jack County had been nearly depopulated by Indian raids during the war, and even now, with a cavalry post just south of town, things weren't much better. The Yankee cavalry had a bad habit of losing a trail, and the soldiers were loath to sign on Southern-born scouts.

"Can't fight Indians with infantry," Sam had told a series of fort commanders. "You've got to outrun a Comanche, locate his camp, hit the women and children. You take them, you destroy a man's will to fight you. And you eliminate the next generation entirely."

It had worked on the Brazos. If the Yank soldiers took offense at such tactics, Sam always found chances to remind them of Sheridan's Shenandoah campaign or Sherman's march to the sea. They got the point afterward.

Sam erased those thoughts as he stepped to the courthouse door. Inside he could hear voices, but neither appeared to be that of Fulton. Sam gripped the doorknob, turned it slowly, and stepped inside. Before him, sitting on either side of a long table, were his brother James and Pat Tyler.

"Sam, what a surprise!" James announced, rushing toward his brother and making a great show of a welcome. "I can't tell you how glad I am to have a visit from family. Long overdue, too, I might add. Did you bring Helen and the children?"

"Weather's a bit rough for them," Sam said, recovering his wits. "Just came in to pick up some supplies, and I thought we could have some supper."

"Well, we'll certainly do that," James replied. "You know

**110**

Pat Tyler, don't you? Judge Fulton's clerk. Pat, this is my brother Sam.''

"Pleased to see you again, sir," Tyler said, gripping Sam's hand firmly. "The judge speaks of you often."

"Yes, we receive a good deal of Judge Fulton's attention," Sam told the young clerk. "I hear good things of you, Pat. And I understand you and James have become fast friends. It's good young men make loyal allies. Leads to a fine future for all concerned."

"Yes, sir," Tyler agreed, eyeing Sam strangely. "Truth is, we're not exactly friends. My cousin Martin went to school with James. As court clerk," Tyler added warily, "I can't very well link myself with a lawyer trying cases before the judge."

"No, I see that," Sam admitted.

"Pat does help, though," James explained. "I'm pitifully short on some of the new state statute books. When the judge isn't in need of his library, Pat offers me the use of it."

"Don't carry it past this room, though," Tyler insisted. "Judge Fulton would raise cain. He doesn't like to think anybody in the county touches those books, but after all, you can't plead a case if you don't know the law."

"Exactly," James said, grinning. "Pat, maybe when I finish here, you'd care to have dinner with us."

"I appreciate the invite," Tyler said, tapping his fingers nervously on the hardwood table. "Another time maybe. I, uh, promised to dine elsewhere tonight."

"Hope she's pretty," James said, and Tyler breathed a long sigh.

"You'll lock up when you go, won't you?" the young clerk asked as he rose from his chair and fetched his coat. "I think I'd best get along now."

"Enjoy yourself, Pat," Sam said, making way for the young man's passage. "Thanks for the help you've extended my brother."

"Sure," Tyler mumbled as he escaped out the door.

"Lord, we sure put the fright in that rabbit," Sam observed as he secured the door.

"He's scared silly by that judge," James explained. "Whole town's spooked, if you want to know the truth. But then it's probably the smart way to be."

"What's this about you lacking books, James? I wrote Olin Preston personally and had him send the new legal texts."

"Pat doesn't have to know that," James explained. "This way I get into the courthouse now and then. Occasionally alone, like now. Willie taught me how if you want to catch a fox, first have a look at his den. Well, we got a different villain to trap, don't we?"

"You mean you've been through Fulton's papers?"

"More than once," James boasted. "Come have a look for yourself."

James led the way past Tyler's desk and on to Fulton's office. The door was locked, but James produced a skeleton key that turned the trick.

"How . . ."

"Isn't just law you can learn in Austin," James explained. "Here are the ledgers. Have a glance."

Sam picked up the twin books and thumbed his way through the pages.

"Fulton would lose his supper if he knew we were here," Sam said as he gazed over and over at the cryptic entries. "What manner of writing is this, though? There are no figures."

"It's in code," James explained. "I haven't been able to break it down, though. Pat knows, only he isn't about to tell. Even if I made sense of it, the judge would just deny it. Who would a federal marshal believe anyway?"

"So, have you learned anything at all?"

"Plenty," James said, grinning. "I've got a whole list of bank accounts. Trick is tying the money there with the taxes he's collected. I'm doing it bit by bit."

"But that won't convict a man anyway, especially when he's the judge himself."

"That's the trouble, all right," James acknowledged. "And why we're not much ahead of where we were at Christmas."

"Not so," Sam argued. "We know the game. We can catch him at it."

"Stealing tax dollars? Sam, even old Judge Taylor helped himself to a share of the county takings. I'd guess everyone in the state steals a dollar here and there. Your marshal friend Coke Lindsay's quarrel with Fulton isn't that he steals. It's that he won't share."

"Then I don't see what chance we have," Sam said, throwing his hands in the air.

"The two of us? Not much at all," James said, laughing. "But we've got help, remember? Just so happens you're not the only one invited to dinner tonight. Baldy Nichols is coming, too."

"The Pinkerton?"

"Me, I use the law to fight my battles, Sam. Baldy isn't quite so particular. He gets results, though."

"Sounds like he's a man that's sure to get along just fine with me, then."

"I'd say so. Why don't you copy out a page or two of those ledger entries now. I'll work on this other book. We've got half an hour. Then we'll have our dinner and discuss our favorite judge with Baldy."

Sam nodded, grabbed a pencil, and began copying out the coded figures. James did likewise. The time passed quickly as they worked. Then James closed his ledger, took the other from Sam, and replaced them in their slots on Fulton's desk.

"Dinner awaits," James said as he waved his brother along. "You haven't tasted good cooking till you get a sample of what Amanda South can do with a bit of ham and some honey."

"You hired a cook?" Sam asked as they relocked Fulton's office.

"Well, she mainly makes her living doing laundry and performing personal services down at Sudsville. But she makes me breakfast and dinner for a perfectly reasonable sum. In return I handle her legal affairs."

"You've got the makings of a governor, brother James," Sam declared.

"Or a judge," James added, laughing.

James had not been exaggerating when he boasted of Amanda South's talents in the kitchen. But Sam was somewhat surprised to discover the cook was a former slave. The black woman was as big as a stove and shaped more or less the same. Her face was bright, almost pretty in a sort of angelic way, but it was her scarred hands and wrists that attracted Sam's curiosity.

"She told me an overseer did it to her," James explained later. "Down in Louisiana. Whipped the flesh off her back, too. It's a shame. Mars her looks."

"Doesn't harm her biscuits, though," Sam noted.

Baldy Nichols appeared near the end of the meal. Amanda filled another plate with food and set it out for the dwarflike detective. Once Nichols removed his hat, it was clear how he'd come by his nickname. There weren't half a dozen hairs left on the poor man's whole head.

"Don't misjudge me, Colonel Delamer," Baldy said as he observed Sam's gaze. "Men in my family lean to balding early. I'm not quite thirty yet, and though I'm the runt of the litter, so to speak, I can handle myself just fine in a fight. With fist or firearms, either one."

"I'm gratified to hear it," Sam confessed. "Now, maybe we should discuss the business of—"

"Not just yet," James warned, nodding toward Amanda. "Best we have our chat over a cup of coffee after the plates have been removed."

Sam nodded, though he was sorely vexed that next half

**114**

hour while Baldy gorged himself. Questions tormented Sam, and he was envious of the lighthearted way James discussed the weather and the prospects for a good harvest.

"If ya'll through, I be leavin' now, Mr. James," Amanda finally announced as James poured out the coffee.

"Thank you, Amanda, for a wonderful dinner," Baldy answered.

"You come again, Mr. Nichols. Always nice to feed a gentleman," she added in departing.

"It was good," Sam agreed as James bolted the door. "But we've got other matters at hand."

"Sure, we do," Baldy said. "Let's see what you've put together, Jamie, my boy. You were goin' to copy out some of the ledger code, weren't you?"

"Here," James said, spreading the pages before the small man. "There are bank deposit lists here, too."

"Just fine," Baldy said, sipping coffee. "Fine indeed. You can make anything you want to out of these scratchin's."

"I don't see how that helps us," Sam argued.

"You don't?" Baldy asked. "Here I heard you was a clever fellow, Colonel. Why, don't you see? We make up our own system to match this fool cipher. Man wants to believe Fulton guilty'll have all the proof needed."

"And who would want to find him guilty?" Sam asked.

"Now, that's the trick there, eh? Paintin' that Yank into a trap he can't escape from."

"Well, certainly," James replied. "But if we can't verify our charges . . ."

"Look, Jamie, I ain't no fancy lawyer nor educated in the way you are, Colonel. I spent my young days dodgin' bullets and arrows on the Kansas plains. Near got burned by ole John Brown himself! In all that time I got myself a lot o' learnin', most of it fast and sudden. I know men. They's no different than a nasty ole catfish, you know. It's not so hard fryin' 'em up for supper. As to landin' 'em, you only got to find the right bait."

"I've done my fair share of fishing," James said, continuing the metaphor. "Picking the bait's the hardest part."

"So, tell me about this fellow," Baldy urged. "How's he talk? More to the point, how's he think?"

For the next half hour the Delamer brothers painted a picture of DeWitt Fulton. As they spoke of the arrogant Ohioan, explained the elaborate schemes, the skillful covers, the talent for bending and manipulating the law, Baldy Nichols began to smile.

"Politician," he finally announced. "Easy fish to catch. Nibble some money, and he'll bite."

"Catch him in a plot," James suggested. "Maybe selling guns to the Indians. Or favors."

"Lord, boy, you got more brains'n that," Baldy complained. "Half the U.S. Senate's sellin' rifles to one tribe or another. As to tradin' in favors, your own cook does that every night. Ain't no lockin' up a judge for that."

"He's right," Sam declared. "Money isn't the answer anyway. He's got that now. You've got to find something he doesn't have."

"Such as?" James asked.

"Power," Sam said, nodding his head.

"Shoot, Sam, he practically runs everything for a hundred miles around," James objected. "Isn't that power?"

"Not the kind he really wants," Sam answered. "A man like Fulton makes big plans, has huge dreams. He sees himself king. Called himself that to my face."

"Go on," Baldy urged.

"He's got high connections, and that's our big problem. But his connections aren't as high as they could be. That's our bait."

"I don't understand," James complained.

"It's pretty simple," Sam continued. "You say Fulton is close to Schuyler Colfax, the vice-president. Well, wouldn't he be better off if Colfax was president?"

"Lord, I'm beginning to see," James mumbled.

"The one crime nobody's going to stand for, the one even his friends will shy from, is—"

"Treason," Baldy concluded. "It's genius."

"We put together a plot to kill Grant," Sam explained. "Not a real one, mind you. Just a snare. Selling it to Fulton won't be hard. Southerners assassinated Lincoln, and there's plenty more who hate Grant twice as much. We say they're working with Colfax, and we get a few witnesses to overhear the judge making his plans."

"Witnesses?" James asked.

"That's where Coke Lindsay comes in," Sam said, grinning.

"We'll need some fresh faces to present the notion," James said. "I know a fellow down in Weatherford who would do it. Out-of-work actor. He's from Ohio, too."

"As for a trigger man, I always did enjoy a bit o' play-actin'," Baldy added. "Be glad to sign on, help the occupation forces smash a plot to kill the beloved president."

"Then it's settled," Sam said. "We get started right away."

"Wrong," Baldy argued. "You, Colonel, ride on back to your ranch. Keepin' you 'round town's like settin' off rockets to warn of trouble. Jamie, you go fetch your actor friend from over in Weatherford. We'll get some telegrams put together, sort everything out. Then when it's time to spring the trap, we'll invite you up. Hate to think you'd miss out on the fun."

"So would I," Sam remarked. "This is one catfish I'd enjoy skinning."

# CHAPTER 13

Ψ

The reason Sam Delamer had never taken to fishing as a source of escape from the day-to-day trials of life was that he simply didn't have the patience required. Oh, he did all right throwing in a hook amidst a run of sand bass, for those fish virtually jumped out of the river at you. But the slow, tedious duel with a catfish lost him every time.

Nevertheless, it grated on Sam considerably to be back at the ranch while the snare was being set for DeWitt Fulton. Even more infuriating was the knowledge that his young brother, who was only now turning eighteen years old, should be the one to entrap that devil Yank. James! Who could have guessed that shy, even-tempered boy could pass the bar after so short a time reading the law. He was undeniably a force to reckon with.

Sam did his best to stay busy those long anxious days. It wasn't always easy. After all, the weather didn't lend itself to exertion, and there weren't enough cowboys around to need a lot of guidance. As for keeping up with the ranch accounts, there was no money to make purchases or to provide payroll either. He was more than a little relieved to receive a short note from James with a summons to Jacksboro.

"How long will you be gone?" Helen asked anxiously as she packed a bag.

"I don't know, dear," he told her. "A day or two, I'd guess. It could be longer, though."

"You're not attempting anything dangerous, are you?"

"That's work for other hands," Sam assured her. "You know me better than to ask."

"I know you, Sam, but I also realize these are desperate times."

"But they'll soon be at an end," he pledged, giving her a parting kiss. "Then we'll do some celebrating to make amends for the lean days behind us."

"Now that's a thought to warm the soul!" she exclaimed.

Sam then descended the stairs and bid good-bye to the children. Edna gave him a brief hug, and while Robert and little Sam were more reserved, they nevertheless noticed the high spirits with which their father departed home.

Sam wasn't to be disappointed, either. When Bobby McDowell dropped him off at James's house, the younger Delamer quickly ushered his brother inside.

"You're barely in time," James grumbled as he hurriedly threw on his coat and a thick woolen scarf to fend off the chill winter wind. "We have to smuggle ourselves into the courthouse while the judge is having dinner. Otherwise he's sure to see us and draw the appropriate conclusion."

"I don't understand," Sam complained. "What have you done?"

"Nothing up to now," James explained. "Oh, Baldy's had some meetings, but the hook gets offered tonight. And if we're lucky, Judge Fulton will offer himself up for the kill."

Sam nodded, then followed James out the back door and through the shadowy back alleys toward the courthouse. James used his skeleton key to enter the building, and they cautiously hid themselves in a small anteroom whose thin walls allowed a listener to observe both the clerk's quarters and Fulton's office.

They waited in dark, foreboding silence nearly an hour

before another key turned in the lock. Three sets of footsteps announced the arrival of the expected party. After a moment of removing coats and stoking the fire, Judge Fulton offered his guests a brandy. Afterward, Baldy Nichols turned to the business at hand.

"I think it best for now if we don't share names," Nichols suggested. "You'll just call each other by your hometowns. And me, naturally, you can address as Texas."

"I come from Columbus," the judge explained.

"And I'm from Cincinnati," the third man said. "Cincy should suffice."

"Now, to business," Fulton said. "You have a proposition, I believe."

"Well, let's say I represent certain figures in the government," Cincy responded. "High up, though not at the top. Now, power's only of use if it's absolute, not borrowed. Wouldn't you agree?"

"Certainly," Fulton answered.

"If a man has but a single figure in his way to the top, he has an obligation to his friends to remove that obstacle," Cincy went on. "It's the first law of politics. And in our particular case, there are many in the southern regions of our nation eager to oblige us. But after Ford's Theater and Father Abraham's tragic exit, it's much more difficult to carry out such a plan. It requires enormous cooperation, and that means acquiring cash."

"That's where you need me," Fulton observed. "I've laid my hands on the ten thousand Texas here mentioned. For this sum, I understand I buy in."

"Call it a down payment. We'll need much more, perhaps twenty-five."

"That's beyond my entire reserve. I'd have to impose a levy to raise that much."

"Does that pose a particular problem, Columbus? You would have two weeks. The general goes on an inspection tour in late March, and it's then we plan to carry out our plan."

"And my reward?"

"Ah, in addition to the undying friendship of our mutual Ohio friend, you would receive authority for all government contracts issued in the Southwest. I include New Orleans in your district, by the way. There's a small fortune to be made just in the riverfront trade there."

"Go on."

"You can, in addition, have an ambassadorial position if you choose. Our friend suggested you might enjoy England or France. In a year, after he satisfies the party radicals of his personal sincerity, there will be cabinet removals."

"I always thought the treasury an interesting department," Fulton declared.

"Then certainly it would be yours, Columbus. Our friend, by the way, has spoken of reviving the national bank. Now there would be an opportunity indeed."

"Indeed," Fulton said.

"Then if everything is satisfactory, I will return two weeks from tomorrow to accept the promised funds. You will raise them in that time."

"There's the matter of insurance," Fulton said.

"Oh?" Cincy asked.

"I'm delivering a great deal of money to you. I need some guarantee I'm dealing with the parties described."

"You saw the telegram," Baldy reminded Fulton.

"Anyone can send a wire," Fulton pointed out. "No, I'll need something in writing."

"You can't mean to be that big a fool!" Cincy argued. "If someone were to stumble across such a document, we'd all of us hang!"

"I'm not a fool." Fulton spoke harshly. "Nor a trusting sort. Unless an agreement satisfactory to my suspicions is in my hand, you'll see no twenty-five thousand dollars. And I expect it to be drawn on the appropriate stationery."

"You ask a man to risk much," Cincy grumbled. "But without your cash, there's little chance of success. I've no choice but to agree to your terms."

"Excellent," Fulton said in a triumphant voice. "Now, I fear I must bid you gentlemen good day. I've work to attend to."

"Good evening, Columbus," Cincy said, stepping to the door. "I wish you every good fortune."

"As I do you, sir," the judge answered.

It was a few moments more before Baldy Nichols, too, made his exit. Then Fulton extinguished the fire, put out the lamps, and made his own withdrawal.

Sam and James remained half an hour. Then, as darkness fell like a curtain on Jacksboro, the Delamers hurried down the street toward the little house on the Belknap road. Amanda, dependable as always, had supper hot and ready.

"You be mighty late this night," she scolded James. "But I see now you got out-o'-town visitors. That be the reason. You men have yourselves a good eat. Amanda got to go tend her other business."

The cook departed forthwith, leaving Sam to discuss with James and Baldy the plans for completing the plan.

"First, I paid Calvin Eustiss, who you know as Cincinnati, his promised two thousand," Baldy explained. "Took two more myself for expenses, and I'll deliver another thousand to Marshal Lindsay to get his attention. The other five we split as agreed, eh, Jamie?"

James nodded, and Nichols paused in his eating to dump the neat bundles of bank notes on the table. He divided the bills into three piles, handing one to Sam, stuffing the second in his coat pockets, and passing the third over to James.

"We agreed not to mention this money to the marshal," James explained. "It's our personal revenge on the judge."

"I understand," Sam said, appreciating the plan more each moment.

"Besides, you'll need to be able to pay the new levy Fulton is certain to make," James added. "If you'd like, you can join us in two weeks for the kill."

"I'll be here," Sam promised.

"Only one thing, Colonel," Baldy said, frowning heavily. "Don't have that boy drive you into town in your carriage. Half a dozen folks hereabouts've whispered your name. Judge Fulton's a fool, but he's not altogether stupid. Take the stage, and get off when it pulls up by the fort."

"Good idea," James agreed. "Don't let Fulton slip away because you grow impatient, either, Sam. Play the desperate rancher when he demands more taxes. We'll have our moment soon enough. That's a certainty."

Sam nodded.

The new tax levy struck Travis Cobb by surprise. When the judge personally rode among Palo Pinto's ranches with the news, he was met with anger and disbelief.

"It's winter now, Judge!" Herb Finch cried. "Hard enough of a time without new taxes. I don't know I can pay 'em."

"Pay or get off this land!" Fulton answered angrily.

Travis happened to witness the scene, and he quickly jumped to his neighbor's defense.

"What's the money to be for, Judge Fulton?" Travis demanded to know. "Another bridge? New lace curtains for your office?"

"Oh, call it a contribution to aid in the continuance of stability and good government along the Texas frontier," Fulton answered. "And mind your tongue. I'm aware of your service in the rebellion!"

Only Sam Delamer smiled as he received the word. It was a great mystery, and the other ranchers whispered a dozen reasons.

"Maybe ole Sam's give up," Art Cobb said. "Or perhaps he's cozyin' up to the Yanks again."

"Could be," Travis admitted. "I don't know what's on

that mind o' his, but I wish I did. A smilin' Sam makes me plenty nervous."

Sam Delamer paid the thousand-dollar levy directed against the Trident Ranch in person, in Jacksboro, the same day Calvin Eustiss returned.

"I'm surprised you managed the money, Sam," a grinning DeWitt Fulton observed when Pat Tyler scribbled a receipt.

"There were a few things left to sell," Sam muttered. "It must make you proud to lay the people so low, Fulton."

"Not all the people," Fulton said, laughing at his vanquished foe. "Just some. You know yourself, Sam, that there are winners and losers in every game. The higher the stakes, the harder the fall."

Sam nodded, then turned away in pretended anger. Inside he imagined how fine it would feel to hurl those words back at DeWitt Fulton.

Coke Lindsay also arrived in Jacksboro that wintry afternoon. With him came a pair of treasury agents and another federal marshal. The four men appeared quite by surprise at the courthouse as Pat Tyler was preparing to lock up that evening. With them came Baldy Nichols, Sam Delamer, and young James.

"Gentlemen, I'm just leaving," Tyler explained. "Perhaps we can meet tomorrow. The judge has left for dinner, and I—"

"It's you we came to see," Lindsay explained. "And the judge, though that will come a bit later."

"Sir?" Tyler asked.

"Have you ever seen any of these gentlemen here before?" Lindsay asked, nodding to Nichols and Eustiss.

"Well, I believe they've been here," Tyler admitted, "but then most everyone wanders by now and then."

"And do you know of any private meetings Judge Fulton has held with them?" the marshal added.

"I'm not privy to such matters, sir," Tyler responded. "I'm just a clerk, after all."

"This is a serious matter, son," Lindsay barked in a threatening tone. "It concerns the security of our nation and the life of the president. Do you know where Judge Fulton keeps his records?"

"Naturally," Tyler said, trembling. "I'll fetch them."

"That would be wise," Lindsay replied. "Hurry, boy. There's not much time."

Pat Tyler unlocked Fulton's office and located the ledgers. Baldy Nichols quickly provided an explanation of the entries which proved DeWitt Fulton to be siphoning monies. More damaging, Nichols showed payoffs to Southern conspirators.

"I don't see how that can be right," Tyler objected. "The judge is a true Union man. I've heard him speak of the rights of Negroes, of how the South should be rebuilt as a democratic realm."

"Realm?" Lindsay asked. "Yes, we've heard that word mentioned. This Fulton sees himself king of all the Southwest, with a personal capital in New Orleans."

"Must be quite a dreamer to think Schuyler Colfax insane enough to join such a scheme," one of the treasury men said. "Kill the president! Imagine!"

"You'll see for yourselves, gentlemen," Eustiss promised. "You can listen in the adjoining room while we discuss the particulars. He's caused to be drawn up a written agreement to the plan. Here, read it yourselves."

Lindsay scanned the document, then passed it on to the others. Gasps of surprise and muttered curses followed.

"I don't much like this. Not at all," the other marshal, a former Michigan cavalryman named Naswell, observed. "What are all these Texans doing here? Can we be certain it's not a plan to remove a patriot from his appointed office?"

"I'm no Texan," Baldy argued. "I served in the Kentucky cavalry and worked for Allan Pinkerton besides."

"I was adjutant for the Fifth Ohio Infantry," Eustiss

added. "These others got involved because young James happened to grow suspicious of certain persons doing business with the judge."

"I knew a couple of 'em from my days in Austin," James explained. "One escaped from jail after shooting a Negro senator. My brother Sam here served under Southern colors, though most of his days were devoted to frontier defense. I asked him to witness these dealings because I feared to trust strangers. Sam employs a considerable number of free Negroes, by the way."

"It was wise to be cautious," Lindsay asserted. "There's no purpose to questioning the loyalty of these men. I think we can satisfy ourselves as to the truth shortly. Mr. Nichols, you and Mr. Eustiss should set about making your rendezvous with the judge. The rest of us should withdraw to the privacy of Fulton's office."

"What about me?" Tyler asked.

"Come with me," Lindsay ordered. "And if you try to warn Judge Fulton, I'll open you up like a tin of beans."

Tyler eyed the jagged knife in the marshal's hand and stumbled along in frozen silence. Meanwhile Baldy Nichols led his Ohio companion out the door, pausing only a moment to lock it behind them.

"Now comes the waiting," Lindsay said, closing the office door. "Until I say otherwise, no one speaks."

Sam Delamer sat in a chair beside his brother as the clock on the wall ticked off the minutes. Twenty minutes passed before the judge arrived. Another ten elapsed before Nichols and Eustiss joined him.

In the beginning the three men indulged in small talk. Then Eustiss presented the promised document, and Judge Fulton turned to the subject at hand.

"I see you entered the correct amount," Fulton said. "Twenty-five thousand dollars. But what of the other—"

"We're only interested in the present," Eustiss interrupted. "It's dangerous enough for me to be here, and you've

126

imperiled others by having this document drawn. Is it your wish to sign it, or did you merely have in mind collecting evidence to use against us?''

''Evidence?'' the judge asked. ''You misjudge me. I'm sincere in my intentions to help our friend.''

''Then let's get on with it,'' Eustiss grumbled. ''So there's no misunderstanding, I want to state clearly what this money buys you. In return for financing the assassination of President U. S. Grant, you are to be named military governor of the Southwest United States, including the rebel states of Texas, Arkansas, and Louisiana, with headquarters in New Orleans. You can also expect an ambassadorial position and consideration for a place in President Colfax's cabinet.''

''Consideration?'' Fulton objected. ''I helped get Schuyler started in politics. He owes me treasury even without this aid.''

''Well, in our talks, he spoke of it as a certainty, too,'' Eustiss acknowledged.

''Naturally,'' Fulton boasted. ''With that idiot Grant out of the way, we can reconstruct the Union along true Republican lines. Military men ought never to get involved in politics. They lack the resolve to carry through their programs. And Grant!''

''That's enough!'' Coke Lindsay shouted as he threw open the doors of the judge's office and burst into the room. ''Treason!''

''Not me!'' Fulton answered, retreating behind Pat Tyler's desk. ''It's a trap! A plot. Look, there's Delamer!''

''Get your hands up, Fulton!'' Lindsay shouted. ''Now!''

''You're not listening to me!''

''Oh, yes, I heard you quite clearly,'' Lindsay replied. ''So did these men beside me.''

''Pat?'' Fulton asked, turning to young Tyler. ''Tell them. I've never in my life been disloyal.''

''To yourself!'' James declared. ''But you've robbed this country of its wealth, subjected the people to abuse and terror. Now it's time for retribution.''

"No," Fulton whimpered. "It's these men. Look at that agreement. See whose name is written there."

"I see your name," Naswell noted. "I'm certain your judges will take note of that."

"My judges?" Fulton stormed. "Mine! Who are you to wave a pistol at an official of the U.S. government."

"*We* represent the government," Naswell replied. "These others are treasury agents, sent down here to investigate a plot to murder the president. I believe we have all the authority that's needed."

"I don't," Fulton charged. "You've no warrant, and none can be issued here without my signature."

"You're a rogue, Fulton, and we won't let you off on the basis of such a fool's argument," Lindsay answered. "Now, if you'll kindly accompany me to the jail . . ."

"I'll go with you nowhere," Fulton cried, drawing a pistol from Tyler's desk and firing rapidly at his assembled enemies. One of the treasury agents took the full force of the first three shots and fell bleeding to the floor. Sam grabbed his brother and pulled him to cover. Baldy Nichols, conditioned by years of tight fighting, dodged the projectile aimed his way. Meanwhile DeWitt Fulton scrambled to the door and fled into the streets of Jacksboro, shouting murder.

In the noise and confusion that followed, shots were fired wildly, and it was a miracle no one else was injured. As to Judge Fulton, the elusive Ohioan helped himself to a saddle horse tied to the hitching post outside the Lone Star Saloon and rode off westward.

"We best get after him," Lindsay told Naswell. "Tyler, you'll tend to the money?"

"Yes, sir," the shaken clerk replied. "What of the man there on the floor?"

"He's dead," Naswell explained. "So now the charge against Fulton is murder."

# CHAPTER 14

Few of the settlers expressed much sympathy for the plight of DeWitt Fulton. Bands of soldiers swept through the country looking for the fugitive jurist, and telegrams spread word of the criminal throughout the civilized Southwest. And yet Fulton managed to elude every searcher.

"I don't much care if he's caught," Sam told James after the cavalry abandoned the search. "Or if he's hung. He's gone, and that's what is important."

"Someone's bound to take his place," James pointed out. "And except for a few dollars set aside, I don't see the ranch is any better off than before."

"It took Fulton four years to get greedy," Sam argued.

"Would it take you that long? Anyway, we're suddenly in a position to influence the choice. I've spent some time visiting with Coke Lindsay, and I—"

"Do you think you're judge material, James?"

"No, of course not," James said, scowling. "If I were ten years older, maybe. I do know it won't be Pat Tyler, either, and for the same reason. But I'd guess Lindsay might have a talk with you before anyone's appointed. He's got the ear of the government after sending them that paper. And he owes us for that.''

"He won't trust me with the job," Sam said, laughing to himself.

"Can't," James agreed. "There isn't a former Confederate in Texas holding significant office. You know a lot of people, though, Sam. Give it some thought."

"I will, little brother," Sam pledged. "I will."

Elsewhere DeWitt Fulton's exit from Texas brought a mixture of surprise and concern.

"He was a crook, plain enough," Travis Cobb told Irene as they walked from their house on the creek up toward the larger place on the hill beyond. "But you knew where his attention rested. The next one, well, who knows what new hardships he'll bring?"

"Ted says they're certain to break up the district and appoint someone to oversee each county," Irene responded. "At least that way no one man will be so powerful."

"Also means somebody'll be watchin' from Palo Pinto," Travis pointed out. "It's one thing to have some Yank yellin' orders from Jacksboro. I don't think Fulton was here half a dozen times in four years. A man in Palo Pinto's certain to take a more active interest."

"That could be good as well as bad."

"Irene, when did you ever know somethin' to be good when it could be bad?" Travis asked. "I never have, especially since the war. Here they won't even let us cast a vote, and they tax us near to death!"

"We'll do all right," she said, gripping Travis's hands. "We have to. There's a child on the way."

"What?"

"I had Jack Trent look me over when he was down last week," she explained. "It's certain. Mike's due to have a little brother or sister come late summer."

"Well, that's real news. Let's get Pa told straightaway.

**130**

Another grandkid! Better than fresh tobacco for bringin' him a smile!''

"Hasn't had an altogether sour effect on you, either," she said as he tugged her up the hill.

"Why should it? I'm goin' to be a pa myself! And, as Pa says, I'm doin' it the regular way this time 'round.''

Sam Delamer spent early March writing letters and trying to unravel the tangled web of titles DeWitt Fulton had woven to conceal ownership of the Bayles farm and other properties upriver. Sam didn't have the funds to acquire the land himself, but he fully intended to prevent Fulton or any accomplice from turning that acreage over to a potential adversary like the Cobbs or Ted Slocum.

"You seem to spend a lot of hours staring at those swords," Clayton Stanpole observed as he stepped into the ranch office one day near the middle of the month. "Your family heritage, I take it."

"They are, but it's not the swords I stare at," Sam explained. "It's the map. I stare at those small squares of property that ought to belong to the ranch, and I lose all patience. It wasn't so long ago I had the whole county on the run. Then that fool Fulton turned on me, and he near finished us all. Bled us dry of funds! Clay, I gaze at empty shelves and bare walls, and I want to hunt that crooked Yankee down and barbecue his accursed hide!"

"What you need's not revenge, Sam," Stanpole declared. "It's aid. Can't Senator Preston help? He relies on us for financing."

"It's not Austin that worries me," Sam confided. "It's local. Another crook like Fulton would be disastrous."

"James said you're in a position to recommend a nominee."

"Oh, sure, but who would that be? I've got more enemies in Texas than Billy Sherman. They won't appoint anyone who

131

undertook Confederate service, and that's most everybody over twenty-five with a measure of education."

"You know my position on the plantation prevented my bearing arms," Stanpole said as he examined the map closely. "I don't have much by way of legal training, but James might relocate his offices nearby. So long as I was provided a good house and enough money to be comfortable, I wouldn't see the need for much in the way of taxes."

"You?" Sam asked. "Clay, you nearly ruined the ranch!"

"Oh, you'd see I didn't harm the county, Sam. You and James. And when it came to rulings on boundary lines and such, well, you'd have a friendly ear."

"You wouldn't be too popular with the neighbors. And you'd surely have to rely on state police to enforce your orders. There aren't any soldiers in Palo Pinto."

"State police?"

"They're most of them Negroes."

"Slaves?" Stanpole asked, frowning. "Well, I wouldn't have to kiss them, would I? I've known some to be quite reliable, in fact. I surely wouldn't have to concern myself with any of them spying on me. Who'd believe a man of color?"

"You know, the more I consider it, the better this sounds," Sam confessed. "In fact, it's near genius, Clay. Now don't go speaking of it to anyone. It's best Lindsay hears it from me, as a sort of surprise. Yes, that would be best."

"Whatever you say, Sam."

"I will need to speak to James. Maybe we should both go into Jacksboro in a day or so. I always imagined we'd have someone from the family in government. Might as well start with you."

"My feelings exactly." Stanpole spoke with a broad smile.

Marshal Coke Lindsay appeared at the Trident Ranch the day after Sam and Clayton returned from their visit to Jacksboro. The lawman was accompanied by a patrol of soldiers and a wagon containing most of the twenty-five thousand dollars taken from DeWitt Fulton.

"I don't suppose we'll ever make enough sense of those ledgers to redistribute this equitably," Lindsay confessed, "but I've done my best to return a portion to each taxpayer. I set up a reward fund for Judge Fulton with three thousand dollars, and I paid Baldy Nichols and that Eustiss fellow five hundred apiece for their help. What's left was split among the landowners, and your share, Colonel, comes to two thousand two hundred dollars."

"I'm grateful," Sam said as he accepted the bundle of bank notes. "I fear the children have grown appallingly thin these past months. We can perhaps buy vegetables and some fruit."

"It's the young ones always take the brunt of hard times," Lindsay grumbled. "You know I only took a small reward myself in regard to this business. Of course, my standing among important people has risen considerably. I understand I may be in line for a governorship, perhaps in New Mexico Territory."

"Congratulations, Marshal Lindsay," Sam said, offering his hand. "I'll rest easier knowing loyal and vigorous hands are at work in that wilderness."

"I sense there's considerable gratitude felt in Washington toward you, too, Colonel. The president himself cabled me thanks, and he requested I extend his heartfelt appreciation and eternal respect to an old enemy. I was also asked to discover if there was anything the government might do to show its regards."

"No, I didn't expect thanks for bringing a thief into the light of justice."

"Naturally not, sir, but I have been asked. It would please the president to repay this debt."

"Well, there is one thing, Marshal. As you know, we've suffered much at the hands of that man . . . Fulton. If I could be assured that another man of the same cut wouldn't be

**133**

placed in his stead, that we would not suffer from continued persecution, that would be rich payment indeed.''

"I can promise you changes are in motion, Colonel. You'll no longer have to rely on a court in Jacksboro for civil remedy, nor will your taxes be levied on the whims of a man fifty miles away. There's to be a courthouse and jail built in Palo Pinto. A judge there will enforce the law here.''

"Has he already been appointed then?'' Sam asked.

"No, there seems to be a lack of qualified candidates. You must understand there's concern about asking for suggestions from certain quarters. Have you someone in mind yourself?''

"As you know, many Texans trained in the legal profession also served the previous government.''

"Making it unlawful for them to hold office now. Yes, that's a true problem. Soon I hope the weaknesses of that dictate will allow its nullification.''

"Surely when wise men again gain their senses, justice will prevail.''

"And in the meantime, might you know a man?''

"As it happens, my brother-in-law has recently come for a visit. He was a plantation manager, but his strong sympathy for Negroes prevented him from taking Southern arms on moral grounds. Perhaps you would like to meet him.''

"Certainly,'' Lindsay agreed. "Is he here now?''

"I'll send Matthew to find him. Clayton Stanpole is his name,'' Sam added as he stepped to the door to summon Matthew. "His father, I believe, or an uncle perhaps, read the law. My brother, you realize, is a member of the profession.''

"And certain to be of help,'' Lindsay remarked. "This is most promising. Perhaps I'll have some good news for you when I complete my present errand and return to Jacksboro.''

"Let's hope so.''

It was a squad of soldiers that brought word of Clayton Stanpole's appointment as Palo Pinto County's occupation officer and county judge. At the same time the bluecoats passed revised tax orders and bills payable in the following fall.

"Who's this new judge?" Art Cobb asked as he examined the figures.

"Who cares?" Les asked. "He's cut our taxes to a tenth of last year's figures. Bound to be a man to know."

"Oh, he seems well regarded," one of the soldiers remarked. "A Louisianan, though not one to talk the muddle of language they use down there. Brother-in-law o' your neighbor, Colonel Dellem."

"Delamer?" Travis asked. "He's brother-in-law to Sam Delamer?"

"Why, that's the name, sir," the soldier replied. "Knows the country, people say. Has sympathy for the people, but he aims to hold the law tightly."

"Sure," Art Cobb said as the smile left his face. "He'll certainly have an eye to our interests, and that's gospel."

After the soldiers left, Art called the family together to discuss the grim news.

"I don't understand why your faces have grown so long," Irene complained. "He's reduced the taxes, and I understand from the Finches he speaks of using the monies collected to build a school open to all."

"He's a Delamer, even if it's by marriage," Travis explained. "And it's bound to be Sam got him the job."

"If that's true, how can you be certain it's a problem?" she asked.

"Oh, it's clearly not a problem for Sam. In point of fact, he's gone and solved all his troubles," Travis grumbled. "Now he's sure to turn to other matters."

"Namely us," Les added.

Irene gazed at Travis as he nodded his agreement.

"Good thing the shotguns are still handy," old Art said as he drew out his pipe. "Sure to be needed."

# CHAPTER 15

Ψ

Rarely was Sam Delamer in so jovial a mood as the day he stood as witness when Marshal Coke Lindsay swore Clay Stanpole in as new county judge for Palo Pinto County. If the ceremony was sparsely attended, well, that was all right. The other residents of the county had a right to view the appointment with suspicion. Sam was already busy drawing up his plans for their demise. Never again would he suffer at the hands of his neighbors! Never again would he watch their amused eyes as calamity befell the Trident Ranch.

With cash reserves once again in hand, Sam invoked changes immediately. First of all, new furnishings—some from Judge Fulton's personal collections—were provided the house. The children had a rare springtime Christmas of sorts, and Robert even received a spry pinto pony. Those hands loyal enough to have stood by the Trident during its hardest days were paid back wages and a bonus to boot. Moreover, Chance Cooper enlisted a range crew from among the idlers at The Flat and the half-dozen soldiers discharged from Fort Richardson.

"Feels good to have a full crew again," Sam declared as he met with Baldy Nichols, Morgan Delaney, and the Cooper brothers. "We can mend the fences, get a handle on the stock, and tend to personal matters."

"Yeah, I figured you to have somethin' in mind, Colonel," Delaney said. "Elsewise you wouldn't be keepin' on so many guns."

"Time to settle up with them Cobbs, I'll bet," Chance told his cousin Matt. "Near burned and starved 'em out 'fore that Yank judge put us on the run."

"If there's just the one family," Delaney said, following Sam's eyes to the map, "the boys and me'll make short work of it. Done it before, you know."

"You can't just ride down and shoot them all," Sam objected.

"Can't we?" Delaney asked. "Figure your brother-in-law'd prosecute us? Don't you worry, Colonel. We'd make it seem like renegades did it. Nobody'd trace it to you."

"Most of the county would," Sam argued. "They'd make sure I never got title to the place. No, I want Art Cobb's signature on a transfer deed. All nice and legal so even Reverend Ames blesses me for my kindness."

"Beggin' your pardon, Colonel," Chance said, "but that's the hard way."

"Not so hard," Sam said, turning to Nichols. "How would you set about it, Baldy?"

"Take three, four months, but it ain't so hard," Nichols replied. "You got 'em boxed in, Colonel. Tight as a cork in a bottle. Nobody I know's ever got hung in Texas for shootin' a man that's come onto his land. Fence 'em in snug. Then cut off their water."

"It's just how we'll do it," Sam told the others. "If it hadn't been for family opposition, I would have concluded this whole business back in sixty-six. Well, I'm known as a patient man. Four years isn't so long to wait."

The others nodded, but their eyes betrayed doubts as to the patient nature of their employer. And as Sam went on to issue orders choking off the creek that watered the Cobb ranch, there was little doubt he now wished a rapid conclusion to the affair.

But even as Baldy Nichols began organizing crews to seal off the Cobb place, the shadow of a greater threat fell across Palo Pinto County. Bands of hunters were combing the far reaches of the Llano Estacado, exterminating the great southern buffalo herds. Moreover, changes in command at the frontier forts had brought about a scarcity of cavalry patrols. Comanche raiders, furious at the hunters and unsuccessful at venting their anger at the bluecoat soldiers, turned instead toward the frontier settlements.

They came as suddenly as had the cyclone of '69. One ranch after another disappeared in a violent whirlwind of smoke and flame. By the time smoke warned the next place, the Indians were already there. Oh, a few dumbfounded cowboys or ashen-faced women and children stumbled into settlements with terrifying reports. But that came later, after the real menace had passed.

Sam Delamer was inspecting the barbed-wire fences his men were erecting along the northern boundary of the ranch when the scouts for a hunting party appeared on the southern bank of the Brazos. For a few moments Sam stood in stunned silence as he watched a pair of bare-chested boys dismount and examine the strands of prickly wire that came to a halt at the banks of the river. As his wits returned Sam silently waved Chance Cooper and his cousin Matt to his side.

"Those are Comanches," Sam told the others. "Think you can drop them both without one getting away."

"Easy, Colonel," Chance declared. "Always carry my old Sharps with me for this sort o' problem. Matt, you work your way down the fence line and be ready to cut off their retreat. Might be I can't get 'em both from long range."

"Hope not," Matt said, smiling with excitement as he buckled his gunbelt and lovingly drew out a pair of matched Remington revolvers. Sam only shook his head and grinned.

It was always the way with the young ones. They hurried toward death.

While the Cooper brothers turned to deal with the Co-manches, Sam assembled the rest of the crew in a circle around two wagons used to carry the wire and fenceposts.

"Ain't feared o' them boys at the river, is you, Colonel?" a shaggy-haired cowboy named Sunderland asked.

"Boys don't come into life grown," Sam answered warily. "There's certain to be others around."

The grins of the others suddenly vanished. Instead their eyes scanned the brush-covered hills and tangled ravines for signs of life.

Meanwhile Chance Cooper crawled up a nearby hill and took aim with his Sharps rifle on the curious Comanches. The boys were shaking the fence and cautiously touching the prickly points of the barbs. One began to put on a pretense of howling when Chance fired his first shot. The bullet plunged through the Indian's neck into his chest, knocking him back against the fence. For a moment the second Comanche thought it a continuation of the prank, and he laughed wildly. Then, reaching over and grasping the limp form of his friend, he shrank back in horror at the bloody mess he discovered.

By that time Chance had reloaded, and the Sharps barked again. The young Comanche must have sensed his danger, though, and he was already racing toward his horse. The conical bullet struck his right hip, dropping him to the hard ground. He struggled to his feet and crawled on. But Matt Cooper stepped out to block the escape.

"I'll clean up the scraps, Chance!" Matt howled as he emptied his pistols into the wounded Comanche.

"Matt!" Chance called in warning.

But the younger Cooper was still firing at his dead victim when the other Indians splashed through the river. A short, barrel-chested warrior raised a lance and drove it between Matt Cooper's shoulder blades. The lance lifted the young killer off the ground until the weight of the limp body snapped its shaft.

"Lord, there's a hundred of 'em!" Sunderland cried.

Sam clawed the side of the wagon and watched in dismay as a dozen Comanches gathered around the slain scouts. A pair of the younger ones jumped down and started in on Matt Cooper's body. Chance, seeing them, opened fire with his Sharps. The Indians gazed up the hill, gave a shout, and set after Chance Cooper like a pack of hungry wolves chasing a wounded deer. Chance slung his rifle aside and fled with abandon down the hill toward the wagons.

"Fool," Sam muttered. "He's leading them right to us."

"Ready your guns!" Chance shouted.

"Guns?" one of the younger hands cried. "What guns?"

Sam stared in dismay at the huddle of cowboys. Not half of them were armed. Pistols, after all, were expensive, and a man without regular work was known to sell off everything short of his trousers. Sunderland and a veteran cowboy named Simms had extra pistols, and they thrust them into the hands of a pair of wary youngsters.

"You'll come to regret leaving that rifle," Sam complained after Chance hurtled a wagon tongue and landed amidst his comrades.

Chance took a glance at his five companions, handed Sam a pistol, and opened fire on the Indians now milling around the distant hill.

"They got Matt!" Chance said as he fired the pistol harmlessly at the distant horsemen. "Lord, stuck a lance clean through him!"

"Killed him?" Sunderland asked.

"Best hope so," Simms said, biting off a chaw of tobacco. "Apt to do some cuttin' on that 'un. Lots o' bullets in that second boy."

"Butcher!" Chance screamed as he tried to reload his pistol.

"You're doing no good shooting at them from this range,"

Sam scolded. "And unless somebody's carrying a box of shells I don't know about, we haven't the ammunition to waste."

"Don't matter," Simms grumbled. "Look yonder."

Sam followed the cowboy's pointing finger to the river. More and more Comanches poured across the water until fifty or sixty gathered on the hill. Simms was right. A single charge, and it would be all over.

You got the devil's own luck, Art Cobb, Sam thought as he waited for the Indians to come. Just when the ax was sure to fall, this happens! First the twister, and now . . .

"Colonel, maybe we best make a break for it," Chance suggested. "They don't seem too sure what to do."

"They'll figure it out by and by," Sam answered. "You can't outrun an Indian on a *good* horse. All we've got are these old mules, and they're still strapped in their harness."

"Only thing to do's stay put," Simms agreed. "We can hurt 'em come the first rush. They might shy away. Not likely, but there's always a chance of it."

"My ma wanted me to be a cashier at the bank," one of the youngsters told the other. "Me, I wanted excitement."

"Got your wish," the second boy replied, grinning. "Me, I never figured to die in bed. Figure Miz Delamer'll spring for a pine box to bury us in, Colonel?" the young cowboy asked.

"Won't be 'nough pieces left to bury," Simms said, spitting tobacco juice at the wagon wheel. "Them Comanches cut you up real proper, Smitty. Might be one o' the bucks'll keep your hair for a reminder. Maybe make a whistle out o' one o' your fingers."

"Won't happen." Sam suddenly spoke with new confidence. "They won't charge us."

"What?" Chance cried.

"Would've done it by now. No, they're fine ones to wail and fight once somebody gets them started, but they haven't painted themselves up proper. No medicine to protect them from our bullets. See! They can't get up the nerve."

The others watched in amazement as the Comanches began to melt away. In pairs, then ten at a time, the Indians simply rode off. They recrossed the river and disappeared.

Once Sam satisfied himself that the Indians had truly left, he ordered the men to hitch the mules to the wagons. He was in great earnest to return to the ranch, and the others were equally eager. Only Chance Cooper ventured as far as the river.

"Got to bring Matt," the young man explained as he set off along the fence line. When he reached the bank, he paused a moment, then bent over and retched. For a moment Sam suspected he might have been struck by an arrow, for Chance dropped to his knees and screamed. Then, after tossing his shirt over a lump on the ground, Chance got to his feet and hurried back to the wagons.

"You need some help bringin' Matt?" young Smitty asked.

"Get goin'," Chance urged, staring straight ahead. "Get goin' now!"

The wagons rumbled along the rough terrain, jolting Sam so that his rump and back ached to distraction. More than once he started to order the pace slowed, but the notion of Comanches lurking over every hill kept him silent. They raced past other hands, shouting warnings and ordering the men back to the house. Even so, Comanches got there first.

It was smoke rising from the hay barn that told Sam trouble lay ahead. Then, as they closed to within a quarter mile of the house itself, two painted devils charged out of nowhere, firing arrows at the wagon and screaming threats. Chance Cooper blasted one, but the other escaped.

"Your ma was right," young Smitty said as he leaned over the arrow-pierced corpse of his young companion. "Safer, them blamed cashiers!"

Sam tensed, fearing other Indians nearby, but as they merged with the main trail they found no Comanche band waiting to block their progress. Up ahead rifles were firing, and occasionally a pair of speckled horses flashed by with their painted riders. But the arrival of the wagons and their reinforcements seemed to set the raiders on their heels.

"Lord, Colonel, they've set the bunkhouse afire!" Chance shouted as he jumped off his wagon and raced to the blazing structure.

"Hay barn's gone," Simms noted. "Lord, look to the house."

Sam was already stumbling toward the porch. One of the black stableboys lay dead between the ready corral and the kitchen door. A faceless cowboy was intertwined with his bare-chested killer a bit farther on. Near the back door another Comanche had been blasted by a shotgun.

"Robert?" Sam called as he stared at his young son, even now holding the heavy gun in the open doorway.

"Matthew's hurt," Robert announced. "Everybody else is fine."

"Son, you killed this man?" Sam asked as he nudged the Indian with a boot.

"Man?" Robert asked. "He's a Comanche."

"And you shot him?"

"He was coming after us," the almost-ten-year-old answered. "Matthew said I should watch the door. So when that Indian tore open the door, I killed him."

Sam removed the gun from the boy's hands and tried to offer a comforting hand. Robert stepped back and stared with hard eyes at his father.

"You were gone," Robert said accusingly. "Like when Charlie got killed. You were gone!"

"I'm back," Sam said, shaking the child by the shoulders. "Now go look after your brothers and sister. And leave me to cope with this madness!"

# CHAPTER 16

Travis Cobb was chopping wood when he saw his brother Les appear on the slope above.

"Best get Irene and Mike up to the main house!" Les called. "There's smoke to the south."

"Smoke?" Travis asked, setting the ax aside. It was only then, with the hillside bathed in silence, that he could hear the faint pops of gunshots.

"Pa?" little Mike asked as he peered out from behind the pile of kindling he was collecting for the wood box.

"Fetch your ma," Travis instructed. "Les, we'll be along as soon as I get my rifle and cartridges. Where are the others?"

"Jesse's turning the horses loose," Les explained. "Edna's helpin' Pa drop the shutters."

"And the little ones? Bobby and Davy?"

"Gone to the river, Jesse thinks."

"The river?" Travis exclaimed. "To Sam's place? They're as like to be shot by a Delamer cowboy as by renegades or Comanches!"

"They've been racin' ponies with young Robert," Les

explained. "I warned 'em, Trav, but they're just kids. Can't even remember the trouble before, you know."

"Sure," Travis muttered as he threw on his shirt and dashed inside the house to fetch his gun. Afterward he helped Irene up the hill while Mike brought along the weathered gunbelt and heavy Colt pistol that had seen action before.

When Irene and Mike were securely behind the thick oak planks of the main house, Travis strapped on his pistol belt, grabbed a polished Winchester rifle in his right hand, and emptied a shell box into his pockets.

"Goin' down to have a look after Bobby and Davy," Travis explained to his father.

"They'll know to find cover," Arthur Cobb objected. "Stay put, son. Your place is here."

"I'll be back in a bit," Travis said, offering a reassuring grin to Irene and especially to Mike. "I been in fights before, Pa, remember?"

"I remember," Art said, scowling. "But this time you don't even know who the enemy is. That smoke's comin' from the Trident Ranch, you know. Most likely that judge's come back to get even!"

"No, it's probably Comanches," Travis argued. "De-lamers just happened to catch their attention before we did."

Travis didn't pause for a reply. Instead he trotted along, grabbed an idle pony, and mounted the surprised animal. Riding bareback, he raced on down the market road before nudging the horse through a gap in the fence. In no time Travis was swinging toward the river.

The mystery soon evaporated. Dozens of Indians were prowling the river, and Travis cautiously remained in a ravine as he studied the scene. The smoke came from the direction of that big house Sam Delamer had erected for his Louisiana-born wife. Only a grave uneasiness about Bobby and Davy prevented Travis from enjoying the notion of Sam Delamer beset by a band of vengeful Comanches.

Travis was in a quandary. He wanted to shout to his broth-

145

ers, hoping they were nearby. But the Indians were certain to hear the call. And if the boys were at the Trident place, Travis wanted to go there, protect them, fight off the attackers. On the other hand, if the youngsters were even now on their way home, Travis's absence placed Irene, Mike, and the others at a disadvantage if the Comanches turned their attention to the Cobb place.

Travis heard a rock strike the lip of the ravine then, and he turned instantly toward the direction from which it came. Not a hundred yards away three Indians rode through a tangle of briars. At the edge of the briars, where the ravine ended in a pile of boulders, Bobby and Davy peered out, their bare legs and pale shoulders offering fine targets for Comanche arrows.

Travis said nothing, though he wanted to scream violently at the foolishness that had put the three of them in peril. It wasn't the time, though. Travis kicked the horse into motion, then halted so that his brothers could climb up with him. Davy took position in front while Bobby hugged Travis's back. Neither spoke a word, but their shuddering arms told a fearful tale.

"Got ourselves in a good fix, youngsters," Travis whispered. "Only way I know out of a hole's to climb. Hold on tight, 'cause I figure we'll draw some company!"

Davy gripped the pony's mane, and Bobby tightened his hold on Travis's belt. Then, with a whoop and a grunt, Travis slapped the horse into a gallop. Up they rode out of the ravine, past the startled Comanches, and swiftly onward toward the gap in the fence.

Travis could think of but one tactic. If he could squeeze through that narrow opening, the Indians might ensnarl themselves in that devilish fence and lose the chance of pursuit. Of course, Travis realized, he had to keep the three of them alive until they reached the fence line.

It was no easy feat, even on a steady horse, saddled and bridled by knowing hands. Bareback was risky at any time.

At full gallop through broken country, it was just plain crazy. But then so was trotting down to a river full of Comanches.

"Lord, I haven't asked much in my lifetime," Travis prayed as he kept the horse a hair ahead of its pursuers. "Just let this little mustang keep it up another mile. Sweet Jesus, I do want to get home!"

"Amen to that!" Bobby screamed.

An arrow flashed past, and Travis instinctively ducked. A second bit into a tree trunk just ahead. By now a half-dozen Indians had joined the pursuit, and Travis gripped his clump of mane and urged further exertion from the little horse. It finally approached the fence, and Travis turned abruptly toward the gap. The pony raced on in spite of the deadly wire on either side. The horse nosed through, though wicked barbs sliced into Travis's left ankle and tore away the leg of his trousers.

"Ayyy!" the Comanches screamed at their horses and made futile efforts to leap the fence. The first three tangled themselves horribly. The others managed to pull up short, but only one continued his pursuit. Travis pulled his exhausted horse to a halt on the road, swung a pistol around, and fired a single ball into the onrushing horse. The animal whined as the lead tore through its lungs, then pitched its rider into the rocky road. The young Indian, the wind robbed from his lungs by the fall, thrashed in the dust as he searched for his discarded bow.

"Trav?" Bobby called, pointing at the Indian.

"We got other business to attend to," Travis replied as he nudged the mustang homeward. The weary animal trotted along, panting from effort, but Travis refused to rest until he passed the gate of the ranch. Finally he climbed off the exhausted horse, ushered his brothers toward the fortified house, and followed them slowly.

For three hours the Cobbs waited behind the walls of the house, peering out the narrow crosslike slits in the shutters. They could see Comanches scurrying around, most of them young and more curious than deadly. They gathered up chickens and slaughtered hogs. One or two managed to catch a horse and ride it off in triumph. But no one seemed interested in attacking the house. Two of them fired arrows at the door, but Les answered with a rifle blast that set their feet in motion.

"What do you make o' this, Trav?" Arthur Cobb asked. "Ever know raiders to act this way?"

"Raiders?" Travis asked, laughing. "Have you had a look at them? Why, they're greener'n leaves in April. Not much older'n Bobby here. Have you seen a one of 'em carry a shield or a rifle? No, the men are elsewhere, maybe at the Trident. These are the come-alongs, looking for a neglected scalp or an easy coup to count."

"They're killin' the hogs," Davy grumbled. "You ought to shoot 'em, Trav!"

"That'd only make their pas sure to return the favor," Art countered. "And it's poor payment for our hogs to shoot a bunch o' boys don't know better, David. Like shootin' you for runnin' off down to the river!"

"They tried it," Bobby argued.

"If we'd run across the real thing instead o' the young ones, wouldn't't've been any tryin' to it," Travis said, wiping his brow. "We'd all be back there scalped."

"Pa?" a worried Mike cried.

"But I don't guess the Lord figured it was our turn," Travis said, grinning. "Savin' us sinners for another day."

"Sinners?" Irene asked. "Somethin' I ought to know, Trav?"

"He come close to cursin'," Bobby declared.

"I think the Lord allows that with Comanches around," Irene argued. "Now, who knows a song? Jesse?"

"Sure," the seventeen-year-old complied. He drew out a mouth organ and began a jaunty melody. Travis grinned as Bobby picked up the tune on his guitar. Davy and Mike joined in a lively rendition of "Uncle Ben's Jug," a popular tune among the dance halls over at The Flat.

"Where'd you learn that song?" Art demanded afterward.

"Soldiers," Jesse answered. "Didn't know the words, Pa."

"Somebody did," Travis said, eyeing Mike.

"Bobby taught me," Mike explained.

"I got the words from Robert Delamer," Bobby said, reddening. "He heard 'em at the bunkhouse."

"Well?" Travis said, turning to Irene and his father. "It's how I used to pick up songs."

"It's for certain we need that church built," Irene declared. "And there better be some knees worn out praying tonight."

"Yes'm," Mike answered meekly. The others replied likewise.

They remained at the big house the rest of that day and through noon on the morrow. It was then Sam Delamer appeared with a band of riders.

"I'm almost glad to see you, Sam," Travis remarked as he stepped outside for the first time in a day and a half. "We've had a few visitors."

"So I see," Sam noted, eyeing the slaughtered animals. "Lots of tracks. Not many corpses."

"They didn't press their attentions," Travis explained. "And we didn't invite them to."

"After all," Les added as he joined his brother, "we don't exactly have an army on our place."

"You're welcome to join mine," Sam replied. "Matter of fact, we're short on steady men, the kind used to fighting. We're hard-pressed to put twenty good men in the saddle, and most of them are young."

"Ought to send some o' them home," Travis advised as he scanned the group. Three or four of the youngest came from town. They carried ancient muskets or shotguns full of birdshot.

"We buried Jack Kilpatrick's ma, pa, and baby sister!" one of the boys barked. "We earned our spot!"

"Sorry to hear it," Art Cobb declared as he nudged his elder sons out onto the porch. "I'll be keepin' Jesse here to help watch the house, but Trav and Les'll ride with you. Sam, don't you lead my boys into no ambush, hear!"

"I know how to fight Comanches, old man!" Sam growled. "And we already know where they're camped. Won't be much effort clearing this nest of vermin from the county. We sent word to the cavalry. They can have what's left."

Travis frowned as he read the cruelty in Sam's eyes. It was the kind of look a small boy has when he pulls the wings off a butterfly for the sport. Men were supposed to get past that.

The two Cobbs located horses and saddled up for the hard ride. As it turned out, though, the Comanches were just five miles away, camped inside a bend of Bluff Creek a hair shy of the stage station.

"This's how it's done," Sam explained to the two dozen riders that reached the Comanche camp. "We form in a line and ride down on them hard. Morg and Chance over there have the powder kegs. They'll toss them into the center of the camp while we drive off the horses. Then we come back and cut down anything that moves."

"You mean the men," Travis said, nervously peering into the fiery eyes of Chance Cooper.

"My cousin wasn't but sixteen," Chance replied.

"Nellie Kilpatrick was just five," one of the town boys added. "They cut off her hair!"

"Kill 'em all!" Sam said. "Ready?"

Cooper and Delaney started forward then, and the others charged toward the horses, firing pistols and shouting like banshees. It was as wild and reckless a charge as any Travis recalled from the war. The difference, he told himself, was that from what he could observe, the enemy this time was a village of sleepy-eyed women and children. The men were off absent.

Life along the Brazos had often been harsh and merciless. So it was that night. Bullets cut through the night mists, striking blindly old men and women, expectant mothers, children who stared innocently at the remorseless men who rode down on them. A small band of young men had been left to guard the horses, and they tried to form a line to protect the withdrawal of the defenseless ones. It was this group that halted Sam's attack and struck down the first cowboys.

"Les, over here," Travis urged as he waved his brother to the cover of a collapsed lodge. The two of them quickly flanked the Comanche line and poured a deadly fire into the determined warriors. Three fell in short order, and two others who tried to rally their comrades were torn apart by a volley from the Trident cowboys.

The battle was over at that moment, for the last guard made a futile effort to escape and was blasted at close range by a shotgun. From there on it was little more than a grouse hunt. Men clubbed little children or blasted helpless grandfathers. One small boy, wrapped in a blanket that would have covered a twin as well, walked solemnly toward Travis with one hand extended.

"I church," the child mumbled, making the sign of the cross. He began to sing a hymn, and two or three others froze and joined in. Chance Cooper shot the whole bunch one at a time. The blanket boy he grabbed by the hair and held up like a carnival prize.

"I'm goin' to be sick," Les cried as he staggered to the creek.

"I already am," Travis added as he stared wild-eyed through the smoke at the madmen collecting trophies from the camp. Moccasins, silver pieces hung like necklaces around small necks, buckskin shirts, tipi covers, buffalo robes, knives, and bows were snatched from the dead and dying.

" 'Yea, though I walk through the valley of the shadow of death,' " Travis whispered. "Oh, you were wrong, old psalmist."

"What?" Les asked as he staggered over beside his brother.

"Look at this slaughterhouse!" Travis cried. "I see it, and all I can think of is that we're next, Les."

"It won't be like this," Les argued. "We won't let it!"

"Can we stop it?" Travis asked. "Look at him, little brother. He's the angel of death in human flesh! He might as well be swingin' a scythe! He's the devil!"

"He's just a man," Les objected. "Sam Delamer."

"No, he's the devil!" Travis insisted. "And he's brought hell to earth this night!"

# CHAPTER 17

Sam Delamer prowled the Comanche camp, his heart flooded by vengeance. He was determined to leave nothing alive in that place. Little Robert's eyes had brought back all the haunting recollection of that other raid, of the little son who lay buried in the family plot. Charlie would never see a third summer. Well, now he would have company. Some forty or fifty young Comanches shared a similar fate.

"Nothin' left but to tend the bodies, Colonel," Chance Cooper said as he pointed to the corpses stacked beside the burning poles and lodge skins along Bluff Creek.

"I'd leave them to the wolves and the buzzards if it was just me," Sam remarked as he stared bitterly toward his hated enemies. "But they'd foul the water, maybe breed disease. Throw them onto the fire, Chance. We're erase them the way ole Santa Anna did the Alamo heroes."

"I figured you wanted the bucks to see what happened," Chance replied. "Learn a lesson from it."

"They know," Sam said confidently as he scanned the darkened ridges beyond the creek. "Be a time 'fore they care to tangle with Sam Delamer again."

"Just the same we best keep the crews armed better," Baldy Nichols spoke up.

"Would have done that anyway," Sam insisted. "We've other game than Comanches to hunt."

His companions nodded gravely, and Sam grinned.

It wasn't long before Travis Cobb discovered who that prey was. For days after the fight at Bluff Creek he'd ridden the ranch every morning, keeping an eye on the new strands of wire that tightened the noose around their necks. The Trident hands never completely hid themselves from view. Some, like that young demon Chance Cooper, hurled threats and warnings.

"They scare me sometimes," Bobby told Travis as they fished the creek a few days later. "They look mean, and they act as if they'd enjoy burnin' us out again."

"Ain't words you learn to fear," Travis explained to the boy. "It's who's behind 'em."

"Colonel Delamer?"

"Since when did you start callin' him that?" Travis asked angrily. "He's never been colonel o' anything! Only fightin' he knows how to do is shoot little Comanche kids and old women!"

"Didn't mean to get your dander up, Trav," Bobby said, stepping back a pace. "It's what people call him."

"People?"

"Robert. We visit him sometimes, Davy and me. Down at the river."

"Be wise to pass up those trips," Travis suggested. "I wouldn't suspect we're very welcome there."

The words brought a frown to Bobby's face, and Travis offered a comforting stroke of his brother's slender shoulder.

"I don't mean to scare you, Bob, but Sam Delamer's got dangerous men ridin' for him. We been shot at before by Trident hands."

"Not lately," Bobby argued.

"Not today anyhow," Travis admitted. "But there's no tellin' if our luck'll hold."

Maybe it was that thought that had Travis rattled. It was the not knowing when and how that made a fight terrifying. Face-to-face he'd never been all that afraid of anything. No, it was the unknown that unsettled a man.

There were, however, a few certainties. One was that to fight back, the Cobbs would need allies. The other need was cash and a store of supplies.

"We've got neighbors that will help," Les declared. "The Finches in particular."

"Ted will help, too," Irene pointed out.

"As for cash, we've got plenty left from last year's cattle drive. Supplies, on the other hand, are runnin' a hair low."

"Time to head for town," Les announced. "I figure Jess and I ought to go."

"You figure wrong," Travis replied. "I'm going for certain. One of you best stay here with Pa to look after the place."

"I can fire a rifle," Bobby volunteered. "And I can drive a wagon, too. Three of us'd stand a better chance than just two."

Travis gazed warily at Bobby, then reluctantly nodded.

"There's something else, too," Travis added. "I don't think it's smart for Irene to be here, not in her present condition."

"I'd guess that was up to me," Irene objected. "My place is with my family."

"You've got family on the Clear Fork, too," Travis argued. "And it would be better for you to be around other womenfolk anyway."

"And what am I?" Edna asked.

"To be honest, little girl," Art Cobb said as he took his daughter's hands, "I'd rather you were elsewhere, too."

"And who's goin' to cook?" Edna complained. "Who'll

**155**

do the washin'? I can shoot a rifle, too, by the way. Better'n Bobby, in fact.''

"She's right," Bobby confessed.

"She's goin'," their father announced. "I'll take the three of you west myself."

"Three?" Edna asked.

"Best Mike goes, too," Travis explained, following his father's eyes toward the boy. "You understand, don't you, boy?"

"Sure," Mike muttered. "I'm not a real Cobb anyhow."

"You certainly are!" Travis exclaimed. "But somebody's needed to look after your ma. Shoot, you've been doin' that longer'n me, Mike."

"Isn't that," the boy argued. "You're scared for me. I lost one pa already, you know."

"Don't plan for you to lose another," Travis said, lifting the youngster up with one strong hand. "But this kind o' fight goes better when there ain't so many targets around for Delamers to shoot at."

So, early the next morning Art Cobb loaded Irene, Mike, Davy, and Edna into a wagon and drove them west to Ted Slocum's ranch on the Clear Fork of the Brazos. As soon as he returned, Travis and Les set about completing their supply list. Then, with Bobby driving the wagon and the other Cobbs riding alongside, they set off down the market road toward Palo Pinto.

Actually Travis had no intention of buying anything at the ramshackle mercantile Lucas Berry operated there. For what was needed, a trip would have to be made into Weatherford. It was risky, being gone from the ranch three days, but Travis banked on Sam Delamer completing his fences before doing anything foolish.

"If he intended to raid the place, he wouldn't bother puttin' up all that wire," Travis told his brothers. "One thing's certain for the moment. The Delamers ain't long on cash or credit either one."

The trip to Weatherford was thoroughly uneventful. In fact, the long dusty journey grated on Travis's nerves. The boxes of tinned food, bushels of vegetables and fruit, sacks of flour, and ammunition cases rattled an unharmonious chorus of screeches and whines. And Bobby's addlebrained singing in his uneven mixture of bass and alto didn't help one bit!

"Remind me to send you over to Sam's when we get home," Travis said as they began the last leg of the three day trip just east of Palo Pinto.

"How come?" the almost-fifteen-year-old asked.

"Because two days of your singin' would surely have those Trident cowboys pleadin' for terms!" Travis answered. "Can you spare us some peace, little brother?"

Bobby only laughed and went on singing.

"Worse'n Comanches!" Les cried.

They were over the market bridge and closing the last few miles toward home when the sun began to set. It was one of those fiery Texas dusks, with violet clouds and the sun glowing orange as it faded into the distant hills. For a moment Travis was transfixed by the view. Then he caught sight of a glint of metal and shouted a belated warning.

"Trouble!" Travis yelled as he pulled his horse to a sudden halt. "Go left, Bobby. Those rocks!"

Bobby was taken aback by the series of barked commands, but he had enough sense to do as told. The boy whipped the team into a run and hurried the wagon toward a rocky ridge a hundred yards off the trail. Les and Travis charged along, hugging their horses as the first shots erupted from the roadside just ahead.

"Lord, that was close!" Bobby shouted as he stopped the horses and sought the shelter of the rocks.

"Les?" Travis hollered as he pulled his mount to a halt. Les, though, raced on fifteen yards until he rolled off his saddle and fell to the ground.

"Got one of 'em anyhow!" a voice called from the thick brush beyond the road.

157

"Two left then," a second bushwhacker answered. "Regular turkey shoot this!"

Travis wasted no time satisfying himself that Bobby was unhurt. Leaving the boy with a pair of loaded Winchesters to answer the ambushers, Travis then snaked his way through the yucca and brambles to where Les lay, breathing heavily, twenty yards away.

"Where'd it catch you?" Travis asked as he covered Les's fallen frame.

"Just above the elbow," Les explained as he clutched his bloody sleeve.

"Almost had us cold," Travis grumbled as he tore open Les's shirt and began binding the wound. "Figure you can still shoot?"

"Pistol maybe," Les said, wincing as Travis pulled the bandage tight and tied it securely. "I can load the rifles."

"Bobby's a fair shot," Travis declared. "We'll hold out. Somebody'll hear the shootin'."

"Sure, they will," Les agreed. "Sam Delamer will. He's sure to send reinforcements."

"Then I guess we'll have to put a hole in a few of 'em, little brother. Let's get you to the wagon. Bobby'll need your help."

The two of them slowly crept across the rocky ground toward their younger brother. The boulders formed a sort of natural fort. The shadows of sundown offered extra cover, and the night that was to follow would give Travis a chance to exact payment for his brother's wound. No sooner did the older Cobbs rejoin Bobby, though, than the firing grew heavier.

"There's more of 'em," Bobby said, pointing to a muzzle flash to the right. "Comin' in closer, too, Trav."

"Hold 'em off," Travis ordered. "And I'll let 'em know they're none too welcome down here."

As Travis filled his Winchester's magazine and stuffed his twin pistols into his belt he tried to get an idea of the bushwhackers' tactics. Apparently they were converging on the rocks from both flanks. It was a good plan. Even if Travis chopped one of the horns, the other could circle around and complete the ambush. Unless, that is, Travis could do some fine work with his rifle.

"So, we're back to this game, are we?" he whispered as he left the safety of the rocks and threaded his way through the shadows toward the left-side flankers. Life lost its sweetness as Travis recalled the massacre scene at Bluff Creek, the piles of butchered federals in front of the trenches at Fredericksburg. There, with the snow stained red, Willie had turned philosopher.

"No general'd ever order this kind o' attack if he had to lead the way," the young soldier had remarked. "And nobody'd join it if he had himself a choice."

Frontal attacks meant wholesale slaughter. On the other hand, this sort of gun duel in the twilight was different. A good shot could even up the outsized odds. Travis Cobb had done it before. He would again.

The first target to appear was a tall, lean cowboy who led two companions toward the rocks. The three of them were not twenty feet beyond Travis. But a fourth man was even closer, meaning Travis had to hold his fire a count as he tended that newcomer.

Travis left his rifle in a natural sandstone hollow and waited for the approaching Trident hands. The fourth man trod on unaware of the deadly blade of Travis's heavy bowie knife. When the man passed within a yard of Travis, the former Rebel jumped out and plunged the knife into the bushwhacker's ribs, turning it slowly so that air hissed between the dying raider's lips, and the man fell in a heap.

Travis bounded back to his rifle, took rapid aim, and opened up on the three men now silhouetted by the setting sun. The rifle hit the first two squarely, but the third managed to scurry off to his right. A rifle shot from the rocks knocked him backward.

"Somebody's helpin' 'em!" a terrified young voice called from the other flank. "Lord, Chance, he's got in behind us!"

"Keep going, you fool!" Cooper urged. "It's just one of 'em left the rocks."

But the rapid volley had unsettled the others. They were only cowboys, the most of them, and unsuited to such labor. Not a one of them pressed the attack, and when Travis got in their rear, too, most of them raced off in panic.

"Got a good shooter's eye, Cobb," Chance Cooper hollered as he sent two rounds slicing through the tall grass near Travis's head. "Just the two of us for a bit. All right by you?"

"Trav?" Les called from the rocks. "He's in those live oaks back o' the road."

Cooper opened fire on the rocks, and Travis fixed the young killer's position. It was too easy, a voice whispered through Travis's head. Too easy. And so, just as he was about to start toward those trees, Travis paused. Sure enough, there was a sound farther over toward the right. As he waited, Travis noticed a shadowy figure taking position so as to catch anyone closing on the live oaks from the back and rear.

Not this time, Travis mumbled. He gritted his teeth and waited. It was nerve-racking, especially after Bobby and Les started calling from the rocks.

"Trav, you still up there?" one or the other would shout. "It's near dark. You gone for help?"

Finally, though, patience paid off. Chance Cooper's slim figure left the cover of the live oaks and approached the other shadowy figure.

"You see him, Morg?" Cooper asked. "I figured for certain he was behind me."

"Could've run," Delaney answered. "Or he could be watchin' the both o' us right now."

The two killers dived to cover the instant Travis fired. His bullet nicked Cooper's ankle, and the young gunman shouted a fair collection of curses in reply.

"You're a dead man now, Cobb," Cooper concluded. "We got you marked."

Do you? Travis thought as he crawled along, gradually weaving his way toward the rocks. Delaney fired a shot that whined harmlessly past, and Cooper added three or four more. Neither gunman had a clear target, though. Travis, on the other hand, could spot his attackers by the sounds of their voices. And he knew something more. The would-be assassins had tied their horses in the stand of live oaks.

Travis worked his way cautiously into the trees, took a good look around, and located no other figures in the dim light save Cooper and Delaney. Ordinarily they would have been enough. Not that day, though.

Travis crawled to the horses and sliced off their reins so that they would elude control even if they were caught. And if that wasn't enough insurance, he cut their double cinches so that the saddles fell from the nervous horses as they bolted from their strange visitor.

Travis then rejoined his brothers in their rocky refuge. As he inspected Les's bloody arm Cooper gave a shout.

"The horses!" he cried. "They've got the horses."

"Get in that wagon now and drive it home fast as you can," Travis instructed Bobby after helping Les into the open bed. "Move like your life depended on it!"

"Does, too, doesn't it?" the young man asked.

"Git!" Travis said, slapping his brother's rump. Bobby climbed atop the wagon and whipped the horses into motion. Cooper and Delaney, despite their distraction, opened up promptly, but the wagon sped along unhindered. Travis could only pray his brothers were as safe.

"You still down there, Cobb?" Cooper howled as he recklessly charged the rocks. "Eh?"

"I'm here!" Travis said as his sights filled with the reckless gunman. "And you're finished."

The Winchester barked, and Chance Cooper spun around

crazily as a bullet sliced through his side. A second tore through his right thigh, and a third fractured his jaw.

"Matt?" the young man managed to cry painfully as he dropped to his knees. Travis then fired a final shot through Cooper's forehead, and the killer tumbled earthward.

Morgan Delaney remained safely undercover. Travis thought to have a go at him, too, only squaring off with hired killers wasn't a good way to lengthen your stay on earth. Instead Travis collected Les's horse and mounted his own. With a shout of defiance, Travis Cobb then set off toward home. Only the cold night and Morgan Delaney remained behind.

# CHAPTER 18

Sam Delamer paced angrily from his desk to the door and back again. Behind him Baldy Nichols and Morgan Delaney exchanged hostile looks.

"Three of our men are dead, you say?" Sam asked, pausing momentarily. "Chance Cooper among them? And another two are shot up bad enough to need a doctor's attentions! How could it have gone so far wrong?"

"Easy," Nichols answered. "You let a boy make your plans, and you sent a fool out to help him."

"Man'd be smart to watch the words he sends my way," Delaney threatened. Even now, hours after returning from the ambush site, his clothes were torn and in disarray, and his fingers bore traces of powder stains.

"Nothing's to be gained by threats," Sam grumbled.

"Not directed against me," Nichols added. "Trouble is you gun hands never understand the subtleties that get a thing done. You had everything goin' your way. The courthouse's in your pocket. The law's your trump card. Then you go shootin' bullets. It's sure to stir up support, maybe even from those Yank soldiers at Fort Griffin."

"It was Chance's idea," Delaney reminded them.

"Well, if so, he paid more than anyone for its shortcomings. I liked that boy," Sam said, resuming his pacing. "Sharp eye, and eager to please."

"He was fast, too," Nichols admitted. "With his hands anyway."

"Never was the same after them Comanches chopped up young Matt," Delaney observed. "Unsettled his nerves."

"Well, I sent a wagon out to bring the bodies back," Sam said, shaking his head. "Wasn't the body I wanted to see, Morg. Now tell me. What do we do now?"

"Burn 'em out," Delaney suggested. "Set their grass to fire."

"And if the wind turns?" Nichols asked. "Or if the fire don't satisfy itself burnin' them and goes ahead onto Trident range? You got less sense than that boy Cooper."

"I warned you!" Delaney said, rising to his feet. "Care to settle this, old man!"

"You two better remember who pays the bills around here," Sam barked as Nichols rose to answer the challenge. "There's been enough shooting for a while. Fires too. I know you're impatient, Morg, and mad from being shot at, but Baldy here's right. It's a different tack needed just now."

"Such as?" Delaney asked.

"Baldy, are the fences finished?" Sam asked. When Nichols nodded, Sam smiled. "Close the road then. Wrap that place in barbed wire so tight a snail's got to beg our leave to come or go. Now, how near finished is that dam?"

"Another day should do it," Nichols explained.

"Then we've got them trapped. They'll receive no help, nor even a cup of flour," Sam boasted. "Won't take long for the creek to dry up. They've got a well, but with summer coming, it won't do the job. I give them two weeks, maybe less. They'll beg me to buy the place."

"And if not?" Delaney asked.

"Then, Morg, we'll listen to your ideas," Sam answered.

"I mean to have them gone before roundup, and that's due to start the first of June."

"Not much time," Nichols pointed out.

"Enough," Sam declared. "More if you two tend to your work."

Travis Cobb might have provided a fair description of that meeting. Even as he helped Jesse unload the supplies, he imagined a sour Sam Delamer scolding his underlings.

" 'Bout through, boys?" Art asked as he stepped to the door.

"Just about," Travis replied. "How's Les?"

"Bled himself white, but he'll mend," their father explained. "Bobby's sure to sleep on his belly a week or so."

"Bobby?" Travis asked angrily. "I didn't know he'd even been hurt."

"Some cowboy shot the seat o' the wagon and put a handful o' splinters in that boy's rump. Mighty pretty sight, all that prime-quality bottom dabbed with iodine!"

"Givin' showin's, is he?" Jesse asked, laughing.

"Mostly mutterin' an opinion or two o' Sam Delamer," Art told them. "Boy's got grit, Trav. Must've hurt considerable, but he didn't yell once."

"He's a Cobb, ain't he?" Travis asked. "They come tough, I hear."

"Hard as juniper logs," Art claimed. "Best kind o' men."

Travis hoped so. There was sure to be need of such men.

He thought so more than ever that next morning when he discovered a new fence erected across the gate leading to the ranch. Every five yards along the market road another fence appeared. Six strands of wire made it nearly impossible to cross. A half-dozen shotgun-toting cowboys lurking in the nearby rocks guaranteed so.

It was three days later that the dams began to have an effect on the creek. Once the rock wall was complete, the water level began to fall dramatically.

"They're chokin' off the water," Art complained. "Shuttin' the road. How's the well, son?"

"Dry as a bull calf," Jesse answered. "I'll get a spade. Maybe we can deepen her."

"We can try," Travis said, gazing anxiously at his father. "But that won't help for long."

"No," Art agreed. "I still got some powder, Trav. Figure you can blow the dam?"

"Don't see another way," Travis muttered. "Take some doin', Pa. You know they'll be waitin' with everybody hopin' we'll be this stupid."

"We could sell out," Art declared.

"Rather die," Travis grumbled. "We'll make a try. Then we'll see."

With Les and Bobby recovering from their hurts, Travis thought to make the try on the dam alone. He couldn't carry all the powder, though, so he agreed for Jesse to come along. They were close to departing when Ed Caffee and Blake West arrived from Ted Slocum's outfit.

"Those Trident hands's watchin' the roads mighty close," West explained. "Ted says you might be needin' some help. Guess we's it. Other three's a mile and a half back, leadin' them poor boys on a fool's chase."

"Ever used a keg o' powder?" Travis asked.

"No, but I shot at men a couple o' times. Guess that's what you'd be wantin' me to do this time."

Travis nodded grimly. He then explained his plan and set off down the creek. A quarter mile short of the Trident fences, Travis took Jesse and the powder off on a wide swing to the east. The Slocum hands went along to the fence and made a show of uprooting the posts and chopping the wire with heavy axes.

"It's them, men!" Morgan Delaney shouted as he roused the five men standing guard over the rock dam. "Open up on 'em. Show 'em the colonel's hospitality."

Instantly a volley of rifle fire sent West and Caffee scurrying for cover. The two cowboys returned the fire, hurled curses, and did their best to distract Delaney's crew while Travis slipped around behind them. But as they approached the dam itself, a voice called out a challenge.

"Who's there?" a young voice called.

"Trident crew," Travis responded. "Come to relieve you."

"There's more of 'em!" the young sentry shouted as he fired a shotgun. The blast was enough to sting Travis's arm and shoulder from maybe a hundred feet away. Any closer in, and that shotgun would have torn him apart. A second gun opened fire on Jesse, and the young man cried out in pain.

"Jess?" Travis called as he tossed his keg at the dam and raced toward his brother. Other shots followed, and he could hear feet splashing in the creek upstream.

"Trav, I'm hit," Jesse howled, limping a step or two before collapsing. "My leg!"

Travis turned and fired his Winchester rapidly three times. The third shell found the discarded powder keg and ignited a powerful explosion. Fragments of rock mixed with fire and wooden splinters in a flash of flame and smoke.

"Come on," Travis said as he helped Jesse back onto his good leg. "Lean on me, Jess. We've got to get clear o' here."

"Best you go on," Jesse said, wincing. "I'm shot good, Trav."

"Come on," Travis said, half dragging Jesse back toward the hole ripped in the fence line. Behind them Ed Caffee and Blake West were firing wildly. Then two deliberate pistol shots split the air. Afterward there was only silence.

"Dear God," Travis prayed as he huddled close to the ground and tried to bind his brother's bleeding thigh. Ten yards away, his demon face dancing in the moonlight, Morg Delaney satisfied himself Blake West was dead. A second clump nearby was certain to account for Caffee's silence.

"You still out there, boys?" Delaney called. "Cobb? Tell

**167**

your daddy to sell out. There's two of you here dead. Can't be many left. And them boys. Colonel enjoys watchin' the young ones plead for mercy. Remember that Indian camp?''

Travis shook with rage, and his first impulse was to fire a Winchester bullet into that laughing devil's skull. But even a bull's-eye would send the others charging. And there was Jesse to consider.

It was vexing to the soul to endure the taunts of Morgan Delaney, Travis thought as he helped his brother toward the damaged section of wire. But there were worse things, death high among them. For himself, Travis wasn't afraid of dying. He'd have his regrets, sure, but everything came to an end. Knowing his death meant Jesse's, too, spurred on renewed effort. And in spite of a loose picket line of watchful cowboys, Travis managed to drag Jesse past and return to Cobb land.

The greatest danger always lurked at that moment when a man relaxed his guard. Travis had learned it often in the war. But it was only human to utter a sigh when he passed the fallen wire.

''There!'' a shrill voice cried, and three shots rang out. The first shattered Jesse's left wrist. The other two struck Travis—one just below the knee and the second in the lower left side.

''God!'' Travis shouted as he fell sidewise. He fumbled for his rifle, but the cold metal of the weapon eluded his fingers. ''Jesse?''

With his left hand dangling limp at his side and the pain from his leg surging through him, Jesse Cobb managed to reach the rifle and fire as a pair of figures emerged from the nearby shadows. One screamed as he clutched his face. The second fled.

''Trav?'' Jesse whimpered as he leaned over his brother's torn body. ''Trav?''

''Get home!'' Travis urged. ''Get help.''

Travis lost consciousness thereafter. When he awoke, the

darkness had vanished. In its place the sun hung high in the eastern sky. A few feet away Jesse grinned from his bed.

"What . . . I was . . ." Travis began.

"Pa heard the shootin'," Jesse explained. "He and Bobby come and got us."

"Sure," Bobby said, appearing as if by magic on the other side of the bed. "Didn't figure a few splinters to be fatal, did you?"

"Depends on where they happen to land," Travis said, making an effort to rise. A fierce pain in his side erupted, and Travis abandoned the effort. "How bad?" he asked.

"Leg's broke," Bobby said, frowning. "Got lucky with the other one. Ball passed clean through. No bone, no vitals, no nothin' got hit."

"Blake and Ed?" Travis asked.

"They didn't get off so light," Bobby said, touching Travis's shoulder with a trembling hand. "Both of 'em's kilt."

"Then it's as good as over," Travis mumbled. "No one's goin' to join the fight knowin' the two who did got shot. And how can we survive with no water?"

"Oh, we got water," Bobby proclaimed. "Well just went and filled itself up like by magic. We're all right."

"Sure," Travis mumbled. There were, after all, Les and Jesse lamed, Bobby hurt, and Travis bedridden. Some army to withstand the efforts of Sam Delamer!

As for Sam himself, he wasted little time in paying the Cobbs a visit.

"Had ourselves some visitors last eve," Sam announced as he delivered the bodies of the slain cowboys. "Bad mistake, trespassing. Gets some folks shot. Others killed. Listen to me, Art. I'll make you as fair an offer as you'd find anywhere in the state. Sell out while you're all still alive."

"That a threat?" Les shouted.

"No, just a truth," Sam answered. "It's bound to happen, don't you see? You can't survive by stubbornness alone."

"Ain't just that!" Jesse added, limping to the door with a loaded rifle. "Come here again and see!"

"You don't get my point," Sam said, smiling. "It won't be me comes next time. And afterward I'll buy the place anyway."

"In a pig's eye!" Les shouted.

"Trust me to know, Lester. Won't twisters or Comanches or the president of these United States save you this time. It's finished!"

Art gazed at his sons, then shook his head firmly. Sam turned and rode away. But there was a sense that he intended to make good his promise. From his post at the front window Travis knew it. It was Five Forks again. Confusion. Defeat. All that remained was surrender—or death.

"I don't understand, Papa," Robert Delamer told his father when Sam returned. "Why do the Cobbs have to go? Davy's my best friend, and Bobby shortened the stirrups for my saddle."

"Come here, son," Sam answered, leading the way to the office. He then retold for the fiftieth time the tale of how Bill Delamer had first come to Palo Pinto County, how he'd fought the Comanches to carve out a home for his family.

"The Indians went away, too," Robert said.

"No, Robert, we chased them away. Only after they killed my brother Stephen, though. And later on, Charlie."

"But what's that got to do with the Cobbs? Davy's papa helped Grandpapa Bill fight the Indians."

"That was a long time ago," Sam explained. "Look at that map, Robert. See all this area lined in black?"

"It's our ranch," the boy answered.

"And see the Cobb place? It's right in the middle. A man can't allow his land to be split that way. The Cobbs will go west. They will have land aplenty on the Clear Fork of the Brazos. More land, and better grazing than what's here."

"They don't want to go, Papa."

"Doesn't matter," Sam said angrily as he pounded the map. "It's our destiny to own this land, to control the whole valley. That's the way it will be."

"Why?" Robert asked.

"Because nature decrees the strong will conquer. We're strong, Son. Besides, we've paid the price."

"What price?"

"Our blood," Sam said, shuddering as he recalled Charlie's small, trusting face.

"I'm trying to understand," Robert said, gripping his father's massive bearlike hand. "But I only know Davy and Bobby are going, and there won't be anybody to play with."

"You have a brother and sister," Sam pointed out. "And baby Stephen won't stay small forever."

"No, we'll all get bigger," Robert said with a heavy scowl.

Sam nodded as he recognized the sullen fire blazing in his son's eyes. Hardship strengthened the soul, lent the heart extra determination. Robert would be a better man for his anger and disappointment.

Sam Delamer almost convinced himself of it.

# CHAPTER 19

Ψ

The Cobbs were sore put to muster a solution to their plight. Travis observed how the family only thought it had known hard times before.

"We're in a cage, the all of us," Les grumbled. "Wired in tighter'n a Comanche choke hold!"

Actually Travis thought there was plenty of room. The ranch itself provided a man opportunity to ride about as far as a horse would carry him in one day's time. The problem was there were too many boulders and trees and gullies to conceal men. It didn't take long for a rifle bullet to bite a man in the side, the leg, or the head.

"Isn't much of anybody left that hasn't been shot," Bobby pointed out.

"Hard to find a pair o' hands to chop stove wood," old Art complained. "Nigh little hope for help, either. Slocum's boys got the point when he took Caffee and West home. Wouldn't be any normal man got himself through all that wire, not to mention them Delamer hands!"

Travis frowned. He could stomach hardship, even Sam Delamer's snide face. But the surrender creeping onto his father's face was enough to tear a son's heart out.

"He knows," Les told Travis as the two of them kept watch on the porch that night. "We're beat, Trav. You can't take ole Sam in this sort o' fight. He don't play it by the rules."

"Rules?" Travis asked. "Never were any rules a butcher and a liar had to follow. Ought to be."

"Sure," Les said, laughing bitterly. "Should be a sheriff to come and open the road up. Or a judge to hear the case fair. Lawyers who'd bring cause without fearin' a shotgun blast in a back alley'd end their days. It's justice the common folk need, and there ain't been a lick o' that since ole Judge Taylor left."

"Was for a while." Travis argued.

"Oh? You mean when Major Willie rode home with you. He was your friend, Trav, and a brave man to hear you tell it. But he was a fool, just like Pa is. You don't outlast a fellow like Sam Delamer. You pay a fellow to kill him. That's how you win."

"Some'd rather lose than turn to such tactics."

"Most do lose, Trav," Les muttered. "That's the point."

Shortly before noon the next day the Cobbs had another visitor. This time it was young James Delamer rode to the ranch. The lawyer greeted his old neighbors warmly, tied his horse to a fencepost, and with considerable agility climbed the fence.

"No point to askin'," Art announced as the youthful-faced attorney stepped toward the house. "Ain't sellin'."

"Tell your brother," Les declared angrily as he tapped the cold grips of his revolver.

"Sam didn't send me," James explained. "I came on my own."

"Oh?" Les asked. "Why?"

"Just because a man shares his brother's name doesn't mean he'd got the same dark heart," James retorted. "When I was little, and Papa was away, you helped me along, Les.

You and Jesse were my friends . . . once. Wasn't me changed that, you know.''

''So?'' Les asked.

''I came to urge you to let me negotiate you a fair offer. A good one,'' James added. ''You've got land. I'd see you take the stock and top price to boot.''

''This is for us?'' Les asked, laughing.

''Yes, for you,'' James insisted. ''Sam will have this place. You know it. I know it. So does he. I've known him longer than any of you. Early on I learned it doesn't pay to get in Sam's way. He'll send in Delaney soon, not to fight you fair or by daylight, but to shoot Bobby when he's chopping wood, or to pick Jesse off when he's toting water. They've got powder for blasting, too.''

''So do we!'' Les boasted.

''Haven't we . . . all of us, buried enough friends and family hereabouts,'' James said in a sort of almost tearful plea. ''For once let's all of us live!''

But in the end it wasn't the sort of fight reason could end. James returned to Palo Pinto downcast and disappointed. The Cobbs readied themselves for the next go-round.

Sam Delamer's patience had run out. He'd agreed to James's pointless errand, but now it was time to conclude things.

''Baldy, you got it organized?'' he asked Nichols.

''Sure thing, Colonel. We be there tonight.''

''Good,'' Sam said, tasting the coming victory. ''Time to warm things up at the old homestead, eh?''

Baldy Nichols laughed at the jest. But there was nothing funny in the deadly gaze of the killer's eyes. Nor in the grim gaze of his employer.

Travis sensed they would come that night. There was something in the air, an unseasonally sharp bite to the wind as it moaned across the land. A man who'd fought often and lived long enough to learn from it grew respectful of sensations and instincts. So it was that Travis spread his brothers around the house, protected by parapets of stone or cross-stacked juniper logs. He took care to pair them—matched poor lame Les and one-armed Jesse in front, then paired Bobby and himself. Ted Slocum and a half-dozen men had crated furniture and belongings and taken them west that morning.

"Irene's got a right to have her husband with her when her time comes," Ted had argued. "There's not a one o' you's whole, Trav. Pure crazed, this stand."

"Like Five Forks?" Travis asked. "All those months at Petersburg with no horses?"

"Didn't win that time, either," Ted reminded his old friend.

"Made 'em pay a price, though," Travis declared. "Will again."

It was an empty argument now, Travis thought as he stared into the fearful eyes of the boy sitting beside him. Bobby, for all his manly sounds and pretenses, wasn't old enough for this sort of a fight. Nobody was! Les and Jesse, well, they were as old as Travis had been at Shiloh. That was no argument, either. Ted was right. It was lunacy! Pride demanded it, Travis told himself, but then pride had buried a million men that decade. Weren't they enough for a time?

The first sounds to attract his attention came from the dry creek bed. Shattering glass and splintering boards marked the demise of the little house Irene and he'd built with such love. Soon flames spat yellow tongues from the darkness below, and Travis ground his teeth.

"Just as well," he finally mumbled. "Wouldn't want anybody else to have the place."

"Trav?" Bobby asked nervously.

"Nothin'," Travis answered. "Watch your right, little brother. They won't come head-on, not with those flames lightin' up their backs so dandy."

175

Travis was right. They crept cautiously among the trees, then started toward the outbuildings. First the coop erupted in flame. Then the raiders ignited the barn.

"Nobody's here, Morg!" a cowboy called. "They've gone and done a vamoose."

"Ain't done no such thing!" Delaney barked. "Just layin' low, holdin' the one good position they got. Won't have that'un for long, though!"

Travis knew it, too. There were too many of the devils, and they were moving in pairs or small groups. Opening fire would only invite a return volley. And yet soon the whole lot of them would be on top of the house.

"Take that one there," Travis finally told Bobby. The fifteen-year-old took aim, and Travis fired at a second figure the instant Bobby sent a bullet through the first one's head. The pair of them dropped like willow sticks shot off a fence rail.

"There's one!" a voice called. Old Art, covering the front window, silenced the voice with a single shot. Rifles answered, and more shots followed those. In minutes the farm was a wild scene of violent ambush. Voices shrieked with fear and anger. Others moaned or prayed. Jesse opened up on a charging cowboy and was shot twice. Les covered him, but then Les himself went down.

"Boys!" old Art called as he answered a dozen rifles.

"Just us now, Pa," Travis answered, offering Bobby a reassuring tap on the shoulder. Travis pulled his hand back in horror. It was wet and sticky.

"Trav?" the boy called as he fumbled with the rifle's long reload lever.

"It'll be all right, Bob," Travis promised as he pulled his brother along a narrow trench and shielded him from further injury with several large rocks. "You be all right?" Travis asked as he satisfied himself the wound wasn't serious. "You can bandage it yourself?"

"Can and will," the boy declared. "Sorry, Trav. I wish I could've—"

"You did all you could, Bobby. Watch yourself."

Travis had difficulty hobbling to the side window of the house, and even more trouble getting over the sill and inside. Art Cobb continued his firing, but the old man had lost his aim.

"Time we left, Pa," Travis called. "The others are all hurt. I need you to tend 'em."

"You could do it yourself," Arthur argued. "Figure I'm so old I don't deserve to die with my own house?"

"This isn't your first place," Travis said, wincing as he thought of the cabin on the creek. "Won't be the last."

"Guess not, son. Did a fair job this time, though. Least Sam Delamer won't get her!"

Art howled and fired off his last chambers, then withdrew toward the side window. Travis covered his father's retreat, then retraced his own steps. For a moment silence fell over the place. The raiders, unnerved by the quiet, waited. It gave Travis a chance to crawl over to Les and Jesse.

"Boys?" Travis called. "Not dead yet?"

"Ought to be," Jesse complained. "Got my other hand shot. Can't even hold a fool gun!"

"Les?"

"He'll live," Jesse went on. "Dragged himself on over back o' the well. Figured he could cut up the ones headin' for the door."

"Well, you won't do much with a pair o' gone arms," Travis said, tightening his brother's bindings. "Slide along back down the trench and help Pa tend Bobby."

"Bad?" Jesse whispered anxiously.

"Bad enough," Travis answered. "Still alive, though. But there's time yet tonight."

"I know," Jesse said nervously.

Travis had in mind to join Les and watch the front door, but before he could take another step, he heard footsteps. He rolled over a fraction of a second before a grinning cowboy unloaded three chambers of twin Colts into where his back had been an instant earlier.

"Well, Cobb," Morgan Delaney said, smiling as his wild eyes drank in the madness beyond the house. "Feel right at home, do you? We warmed her up real proper. Was the colonel's notion."

"Colonel go to hell," Travis said, reaching for his pistol. Delaney fired, and Travis drew his hand back. A neat slice was torn across the back of his hand.

"I want you to watch her burn," Delaney explained. "Then we'll have a little fast draw maybe."

"Hell we will," Les Cobb barked, firing a pair of shots through Delaney's back. The gunman made a half turn as he dropped to one knee, then searched in vain to locate Les. Then, coughing blood, Delaney violently crashed to the ground and breathed a final anguished breath.

"Fine job," Travis called as he sought cover on the rocky ground.

"Smell somethin'?" Les then called.

Travis sniffed and froze. Up ahead, resting against the floorboards of the porch, were two powder kegs. Their fuses were burning fast and furious, but Travis recognized there was half a minute left of each. He flew toward the door, dragging his aching leg along, and pulled the heavy kegs away.

"I got more!" a cruel voice called as Travis pulled the first fuse and tossed it aside. "Plenty!"

Travis stared at the second fuse. Were fifteen seconds, then less, left. It was blind rage brought him to his feet, and a lifetime's anger lent his shoulders power as he tossed that keg toward the sound of the raider's cackle.

"Lord, scat!" Baldy Nichols shouted as the powder keg seemed to fly on its own wings. Raiders ran this way and that. Nichols made a break to his right, but the long tails of his coat caught in the nook of a juniper branch and held him prisoner. "Lord God Almighty!" Nichols screamed as the keg hurried toward a resting place beside the very tree. There was a moment of agonizing wriggling in an effort to free himself from coat or branch. Then the keg struck, and Baldy uttered an inhuman horrific screech.

Travis was burying himself in the rocks when the first explosion struck downward and uplifted the tree. He was glancing back when a second yellow fireball shattered the tree like a brittle glass window and disintegrated Baldy Nichols in the same instant. Another explosion, and another followed, for the extra kegs had been stacked close by, and every one of them ignited in turn, tossing rocks and trees and, yes, men, in a dozen directions.

"It's the end of the world!" a Trident cowboy proclaimed.

"Lord help us all," another prayed.

Travis struggled back to locate his father and brothers. Les followed. Even shielded from the worst of the blast, the two elder brothers bled from rock and wooden splinters showered by the blasts.

"Pa, they're gettin'," Bobby mumbled. "Runnin'!"

"What now?" Les asked.

"Now?" Art asked as he gazed at his tired, bleeding sons. "Now it's over."

# CHAPTER 20

Ψ

Sam Delamer appeared early that next morning with three wagons to help clear away the debris.

"I heard you had trouble, Art," Sam said, grinning in an almost polite manner. "Brought you some food and drink. Sheets of cloth for bandage. Looks like you boys had a bad time of it."

"Seen Baldy?" Les asked. "Might be floatin' past the moon any minute now."

"Gave as good as we got," Art boasted. "Come along inside, Sam. Been a time since you come for a real visit."

"Thank you, Art," Sam said, pulling his wagon brake, waving his armed companions off, and following Art inside the glass-spattered house.

The two old adversaries sat on either side of an old wooden chessboard grown yellow through use and time.

"I used to play Big Bill on this board," Art explained, both to Sam and to his sons. "Taught him to play back in the old days, and he brought the board with him on the long walk to Buffalo Bayou. Took ole Santy Anny there, boys. And Bill beat me the first time the night before."

"He told me," Sam said, grinning and nodding at the

same time. "Then he sent me over to play you when it was my turn to learn."

"Wasn't any fun with you, Sam," Art said, fingering his king. "You spend so much blamed time swappin' off pawns and usin' this piece and that. All of it's deception. A man like that's always beat by a stubborn, head-on ole cuss like me or your pa!"

"He's dead, Art," Sam said, moving a pawn. "And I've won."

"Have you, Sam? Won what? Some land? Hell, boy, I'd sold you the land in sixty-four if you'd come over, told me your plans, asked me man to man. Piece o' land never mattered so much 'cept when it was nuzzled up alongside to Bill Delamer. Land alongside a fellow like that was worth somethin'. Now's just dust stretched out over rock."

"You fought a long time to keep it, didn't you?" Sam asked.

"That what you think?" Art asked. "No, Sam, I fought to keep my boys' respect and my family's honor. Ole Willie'd understand that. He knew. You, no, you murder babies 'cause you lost one o' yours long years ago."

"You've got something I need, Art."

"Know that, Sam. But my name on a paper won't give you what you need. Only what you want. Send James down to see me once I get settled on the Clear Fork. I won't make it hard on you."

"You already have."

"Did I?" Art asked, smiling. "Well, thank you for that at least, Sam. Sam Houston Delamer. Was ever a child more misnamed? Should've been Santa Anna Delamer. Called himself Emperor of the West, you know."

"Napolean of the West," Sam corrected.

"You're right, son. I never was as good at those book sort o' things. Ellie had the learnin' in this clan."

"Anything else?" Sam asked. "Need wagons to load your things?"

"Got 'em all hitched and ready, I see," Les noted.

"Maybe your men could give us a hand totin' things," Art added. "My boys got shot some, you know."

"Be happy to oblige," Sam said, grinning again. "This is easier than I dreamed, Art. You're being a gentleman about it, aren't you?"

"I never been one o' them," Art said, scowling. "No, you gentlemen ruint the country and the state. And you'll do it again, I dread. I won't live to see it, thank the Lord."

"Indeed," Sam agreed.

"But some will, Sam Delamer. Like Trav here. Won't be so far he won't be a burr under your saddle, I'm bettin'."

"That's none too healthy," Sam warned.

"I'm still breathin'," Travis barked. "Could be somebody else is, too. He used to have a sayin', that brother o' yours, Sam. World turns. Remember it. You've got a lot of enemies and few friends. Time's come before when you welcomed a neighbor's help. Now you've got just yourself."

"I manage just fine, thank you," Sam replied.

"We'll take our stock and the horses a bit later," Travis went on to say. "Then you can wrap your snarled wire over your throat for all I care. Devil take you, Sam Delamer!"

Travis quivered with rage as he stared at the charred remnant of the cabin, at the pain on his brothers' faces.

"Perhaps we'll cross paths again one day," Sam told them. "I'll give you a week to move the stock."

"You best hope to take the far road," Travis warned. "Live longer not to crowd paths."

"Sure," Sam said, laughing as he took a seat in a carriage that had trailed the wagons. The young black driver turned around and slowly whipped the horses into an easy trot. Art began supervising the removal of the family possessions, those that were left. Travis sat on the steps and closed his eyes a moment. He could see Irene's anxious eyes watching him ride to her. Mike would climb onto his father's shoulder, and they would be one again.

Sam Delamer walked with his boy Robert along the creek where the scarred hole marked the powder explosion. Behind them men uprooted posts and restrung wire in prickly bundles.

"See there," Sam said, pointing out the ashes of the Cobb home. "Old Art burned it himself, I understand. See where trees and grass are already growing over it, how the earth is pounding the lumps flat? Nature doesn't like lone things, like this ranch in the center of our holdings. It pounds 'em flat. Erases them from memory."

"Mr. Cobb once carved me a wooden hawk, Papa," Robert explained. "I remember that."

"Better to forget," Sam argued. "Times change, and men have to grow with them. We've already stamped the far posts with the brand."

"The Trident Brand," the boy muttered.

"That's right, son," Sam said, lifting the boy off the ground a moment. He'd grown heavy, though, and Sam couldn't hold him long.

"I've got nobody carves me things now, Papa," Robert said, gazing at his shoes. "I saw Bobby a while back, but he wouldn't even look at me. He got shot, you know. Shot bad, I heard. Now I don't have anybody to race horses with me. Nor fish or swim with."

"Your brothers . . ."

"Are little!" Robert shouted. "You know Mama's spoken of sending me off to school. In New Orleans maybe."

"That was to be later. You're young for that now."

"I'd *like* to go now, Papa. Maybe I can learn some things there. Maybe I can even understand how to cheat my neighbors and shoot my friends. Even my brothers!"

"Robert, stop that!" Sam shouted, shaking the boy hard.

"Want to hurt me, too, Papa? It's not hard. Go ahead. Shoot somebody else I like."

"Robert, you don't understand this. When you're older—"

"No!" the boy yelled. "I don't want to understand, Papa. I only want to go to New Orleans."

The youngster turned and stalked off, leaving Sam to stare in solitude at the scarred landscape.

"He isn't at all like Charlie," Sam said, frowning. "But he's what I've got."

Gazing back at the old Cobb ranch, now swallowed by its larger neighbor, Sam half choked. He should have tasted something akin to satisfaction, delight even. It reminded him of the time Willie had fetched home the first prickly pear of the season. It had been a brilliant breath of color on that dull, opaque landscape. Sam had snatched it and eaten the thing whole. Beauty and satisfaction were nothing, and it had only tasted like a prickly pear.

"Howdy, Colonel," Pete Simms called as he helped himself to a dipper of water from the now-flowing creek. "Be roundup time soon."

"Sure," Sam agreed. "Branding before that."

"Always work to do," Simms said, shaking his head. "But it keeps us ole gray heads out o' mischief, don't it?"

"Sure," Sam said, trying to manage a smile for the old cowboy.

It was, after all, true that other work awaited him. And Robert? He would come around once the sting wore out. They always did, even Willie.

There was a rustling in the junipers, and Sam grew suddenly cold. Glancing back, he saw the dark outline of a rider, a tall, blond man wearing a broad gray cavalry hat.

"No!" Sam called, rubbing his eyes. The ghost vanished then, and there was only the sound of the men tearing out the fence posts. That and the nervous tapping of Sam Delamer's boot.

# ABOUT THE AUTHOR

G. Clifton Wisler comes by his interest in the West naturally. Born in Oklahoma and raised in Texas, he discovered early on a fascination for the history of the region. His first novel, *My Brother, the Wind*, received a nomination for the American Book Award in 1980. Among the many others that have followed are *Thunder on the Tennessee*, winner of the Western Writers of America Spur Award for Best Western Juvenile Book of 1983; *Winter of the Wolf*, a Spur finalist in 1982; and Delamer westerns *The Trident Brand, Starr's Showdown, Purgatory, Abrego Canyon, The Wayward Trail, South Pass Ambush, Sweetwater Flats*, and *Among the Eagles*. In addition to writing, Wisler frequently speaks to school groups and conducts writing clinics. He lives in Plano, Texas.